I0782235

Living In Flohio

Written & Illustrated

by

David Phillip Parks

Published by: Telemachus Press, LLC
7652 Sawmill Road
Suite 304
Dublin, Ohio 43016
http://www.telemachuspress.com

ISBN 978-1-951744-91-5 (Hardback)

Ver. 2022.02.23

Book illustrations created by Pixelmator graphics app (version 3.4.2) and Apple Magic Mouse.

In loving memory of my dad, Phil.

Thank you, Mom, for your love and support all our lives.

And to my sister, Katie—thank you for the many great adventures we've had.

A special thank you to Jay, Jen, Ashley, Ian, Steve, Diana, the regions of Siesta Key, Sarasota, and Tampa, Florida, and Northeast Ohio/Western Pennsylvania for making this story possible.

A note to the reader: travel, learn, meet tourists, know locals, appreciate nature, and write your stories!

Living In Flohio

David Phillip Panks '20

When I was a boy, I lived in the best place a kid could want: a small town surrounded by rolling hills, woods, fields and streams. There were just enough people nearby to make things interesting and fun, and rural enough to make it a challenge; things weren't given to us and often we had to be creative to make things worth doing.

My mom and dad are wonderful people and wanted my sister and me to grow up in a small town, but close enough to a larger city, which is where they grew up and where my grandmas and grandpas lived. Life in northeast Ohio was great—we had all the seasons, many sports and activities to do, and lived in a neighborhood with many nice families nearby.

I had it made living there, and as I grew older and explored more, I had lots of ways to spend my free time after school and was never bored. In many ways, I felt like I was the luckiest kid in the world, because I knew everything about my world—life in a small town was everything that I needed, and I was pretty sure most other people lived much the same way I did. I knew what I saw, and with my trusty bike, I saw it all. I knew the best trails to ride, the best trees to climb, the best ponds to fish—and it didn't matter if I were with some friends, my sister, or by myself, everyday was an adventure. As long as I got my schoolwork and house chores done, I was free to plan my days any way the weather permitted. I was happy knowing the world … or so I thought. That all changed one evening when I went home for supper.

After spending the day hiking the field behind our house, I hoped my mom was making tasty spaghetti and meatballs, Italian bread, fruit and salad, and ice cream for dessert. My dad worked hard to provide for us, but he also enjoyed being home with us, and was the funniest man I knew. He liked making us laugh and would often change words to make them sound funny, so when he came home from work that day, he playfully asked Mom, "Honey, I think we should have some BASKETTI!"

Mom already had supper ready; she has the ability to know what we want before we even know. As we all sat down at the table, Dad had an idea and let us know, "Hey Betty, now that the kids are about done with school, I say let's do something different—let's go on a real vacation … someplace far away … and fly there on a big jet airplane … how 'bout a beach in Florida—let's DO IT!"

Mom seemed to really like that idea, and as she brought the food to the table, she was smiling and agreed, "That's a great idea, Honey—it's time to fly to a tropical beach paradise! I've been reading about a nice family destination called Siesta Key in Sarasota, Florida—maybe we should go there!"

Mom and Dad had lived many places around the country, but my sister and I had only been on short day trips near home. I loved looking at maps, and quickly got a map of Florida. Katie and I had fun trying to find Sarasota and its famous islands in the Gulf of Mexico.

During that week, we finished up school, packed three suitcases with light clothes and got ready for our first plane ride to someplace hot, sandy, and unknown—and we couldn't wait! On the morning of our trip, we woke early and drove a half hour to the Pittsburgh International Airport to catch our nonstop flight to Tampa, Florida, where we would get our rental car and drive south to Siesta Key.

As we drove through the foothills of the Allegheny Mountains in western Pennsylvania, traffic started getting heavy as we approached the airport. We carefully read all the signs over the highway so we could be in the correct lane to get to the departures section of the airport terminal. Once we saw a large jet flying right over the trees, we knew we were almost there.

The hills soon parted, and spread in front of us was a massive complex—the biggest I'd ever seen: two large terminals, a major hotel, a gigantic parking lot filled with thousands of cars and trucks, and a huge network of highways that seemed to go all around the airport. I'm glad I was too young to drive, but Dad did it all fine with Mom helping him get to the right exit lanes that went to the long term parking lots.

We parked our car, loaded onto a shuttle bus, and quickly went to the main departure terminal front doors. The entire time I couldn't stop staring at the large jets soaring over our heads taking off or landing—it was absolutely amazing! I couldn't believe how something so big could roar up into the sky like that, so Dad began explaining how the jet engines push the planes so fast that the air around them lifts them up. Katie and I sure were excited, but I was getting a little nervous too. We then checked our bags, went through security, rode an underground tram through a tunnel, and arrived at the gate terminal along with thousands of other people all going somewhere.

UPMC

We then had some time to relax and talk at our gate. Soon, we loaded into our plane that was going to Tampa's airport. I watched the terminal roll away as we began taxiing to the proper runway for takeoff. The engines began roaring and I felt my body being pressed back into my seat. Mom and Dad were sitting behind us, and Dad leaned forward so we could hear him, "Look out the window as we take off!"

Buildings, trucks, lights, and trees were going by the windows really fast now, and in a moment the plane tilted up and I felt the tires leave the runway—and everything felt smooth as the air carried us up into the clouds.

I sat at the window nearest the wing and carefully watched the little flaps move, and how the plane rolled from one side to the other. We seemed to do a big circle as we climbed higher, taking us near downtown. The plane rolled to the right slightly, and I looked down the wing and saw a sight that changed me.

I gazed down from over a thousand feet high to the incredible Pittsburgh skyline, bridges, rivers, parks, stadiums, boats, highways, and distant towns, neighborhoods, and universities. I saw countless tiny cars and trucks slowly moving about the rope-like highways. I realized there were thousands of people in all those skyscrapers, but the buildings didn't look so big anymore, and all the houses and businesses looked like little squares. Dad then said from behind me, "You're looking at over half a million people right now, Son … do you see anybody down there?!"

In a few moments we'd traveled along downtown, and I realized I hadn't seen one person—I knew people were everywhere, and yet they were so small I couldn't actually see any of them. Compared to Pittsburgh, I started realizing just how small my little town was. Did anyone see me on the ground in the farmer's field when they flew over my little town?

UPMC
FederatedInd
K&L GATES

Even though my seatbelt was tightly fastened, I tried to lean forward to look for people on the ground. I had to really squint, but I was just able to make out tiny little specks around the fountain at Point State Park, where the Monongahela River joins with the Allegheny River to form the Ohio River. The specks were people enjoying the park, and boy were they small compared to the buildings—which were also becoming smaller by the moment as we climbed higher into the sky.

Seeing how small people were made me think about all the workers in the buildings, the families in all those neighborhoods, the students and teachers at the universities and museums. They were all going about their day—everybody doing something different and probably looking forward to a meal soon. As we soared higher past downtown, the metropolitan area spread out as far as I could see, and Dad said, "We're flying over about two and a half million people now" … all I could think was 'WOW' … and I hoped they were all having a good day.

Soon we were climbing into the fluffy clouds over the northern part of the city, leaving downtown to fade in the distance. The pilot came on the speaker and said we were about 5,000 feet in altitude—almost a mile high! Dad then said, "Get ready … we're going to 40,000 soon!" as he chuckled to himself.

Katie did some quick math in her head, "Dave, that's like 8 times higher than we are right now—imagine that!"

Then Dad jumped in again from behind my seat, "And don't forget … we'll be going over 500 mph at that height … what do ya think about that!" as he and Mom happily giggled to each other.

Katie said, "Yeah, Dad said that's about 3 times faster than we're going now—this is so much better than any roller coaster we've ever been on!"

This day was already unlike any I'd had in my whole life—I couldn't even imagine what was to come!

Soon we were above the little fluffy clouds, and the sky was turning a deep blue. At about 25,000 feet, the countryside looked like rolling moss, the Allegheny Mountains looked like small bumps, and semi trucks looked like specks of color that weren't even moving along the long ribbon-like interstate highways. Katie gave me a stick of gum to chew; she knew that chewing it would help our ears not hurt with the air pressure change ahead. It seemed to work, as my ears started popping and felt better. People were talking, laughing, sleeping, and some flight attendants went up and down the aisle and gave out drinks and snacks. It was like a big party up in the sky.

In about a half hour of flying, the pilot came on the speaker again and said we had climbed all the way up to 40,000 feet, and were going over 500 mph now, and hoped we were enjoying the flight. We flew over the Blue Ridge Mountains, and then the entire city of Atlanta—which looked like a bunch of little squares all spread out to the horizon. Dad leaned forward and said, "That's about 6 million people you're zip'n over, kids—and we look like a little dot in the sky to them—think about that!" as he chuckled again.

I started wondering what my friends were doing back home, when we started approaching some very high looking storm clouds to our south, and as we got closer, I realized they were higher than we were flying. Dad noticed them too from his window, "Check those out—those are thunderheads probably over 50,000 feet … look's like we're go'n straight into 'em. Get ready for some bumps, kids!" Then the pilot came on again and told us to prepare for a little turbulence as we flew through some storms.

David Phillips

As we descended, my ears started hurting, so I chewed some more gum. Soon, we were breaking through the storms and I saw another amazing sight—a huge lightening bolt shot down to downtown Tampa below us, all while the sun was shining over Tampa Bay, St. Petersburg, and the Gulf of Mexico in the distance. I couldn't believe what I was seeing—it was unbelievable! But I hardly heard the thunder over the jet engines winding down, and the landing gear locking into position. The pilot then said we were going to be landing in about ten minutes, and to make sure our seat belts were fastened. I couldn't believe we were landing already—we'd only been flying for 2 hours!

I was so amazed at our flight, and I realized I'd been staring out the window almost the whole trip. My neck was getting sore from looking to the right for about a 1,000 miles. I didn't mind though, because we just had an incredible journey! And as the plane descended over Tampa Bay, we banked sharply to the right, and I could see large ships, sail boats, speed boats pulling water skiers—it was so cool to see all the different kinds of boats. The boaters seemed to know the storms were moving farther inland.

As we descended, I could clearly see all the activity going on in Tampa. It looked like a beautiful and tropical city. Soon, we were zipping over many palm trees, crowded freeways, and buildings of all shapes and sizes. In a few moments, the ground came rushing up as the runway guided us for a touchdown. I saw the wing changing shape with the flaps, and then I felt the large tires smoothly touch the pavement while the nose came down. As the plane went down the runway, a sudden roar came from the engines making Katie and me lurch forward against our seat belts. Dad said, "Did ya feel that, kids? That's the power of the reverse thrust!"

The palm trees slowed down quickly as they went by the window, and the plane turned onto another runway and headed to the main arrival terminal.

Then a flight attendant came over the speaker, "Welcome to Tampa! It's a balmy 90 degrees today, and we hope you enjoy your stay!"

She then said they would be departing for Washington D.C. next. They had several flights lined up all day long and into the night—and they did this everyday—I couldn't imagine that! I needed a rest after one flight, and was wondering if my head was going to be stuck looking to the right because of my sore neck … but it was worth it!

Katie smiled down at me and poked me playfully in the ribs, "See, wasn't that fun? I told you not to be scared!"

She was right, but I stood up for myself, "Hey, we just went across the country in 2 hours, higher than Mt. Everest, and twice as fast as a drag racer—it was fun and scary… gimme a break!" I said smiling back at her, then poked her in the rib, making her giggle.

Everyone stood up and grabbed bags out of the overhead bins, got in line, and walked up to the main door by the cockpit. Dad leaned down, "Look inside the cockpit—all those buttons, screens, and the yoke—WOW…you gotta be the man to be in there!" He was right, the two pilots sure had a lot to do, and know, to get us all down there safely.

Tampa's airport was huge and very crowded with every kind of person you could imagine. Many of them were speaking different languages, and I liked listening to all of them. We then had to pick up our luggage at a moving carousel with many of the people on our flight. After we got our luggage, we picked up our white rental car, and Mom gave the man helping us a nice tip, which made him happy.

"Have a great time in Florida!" he said, smiling, and waved as we drove away.

David Phillip Panko

First, we had to get on the right freeway to go over to St. Petersburg across Tampa Bay. Going across the causeway took a while because the bay was large. About fifteen minutes later, we drove into St. Petersburg; then turned south, and were eventually going to cross a huge bridge in the distance. I'd never seen a bridge that big before.

Mom said, "Look, it's the Sunshine Skyway Bridge; it's going to take us back over the bay to Bradenton, and then we'll be on Interstate 75 until Sarasota."

As we approached, the cars and trucks looked like little toys going over it. Then Dad suddenly pointed out the window, "Hey check THAT out—it's a cruise ship!"

Going under the biggest bridge I'd ever seen was the biggest ship I'd ever seen. The ship was about 15 stories tall, and seemed very long. This day was getting better by the moment…it was hard to believe!

As we were driving up the bridge, Mom noticed all the long cables supporting it. Katie opened the window and took a picture of the bridge with the ship passing below, and the colorful clouds beyond. Everything was so beautiful, we just shook our heads as we passed over the peak of the bridge, and the ship began passing below us.

Dad said, "That ship could have 6,000 people on it—that's 3 times our town! Looks like they're going on a sunset cruise, maybe go'n down to Jamaica, Aruba, Bahamas, then return and dock in Miami on the east coast."

As the ship passed under the bridge, we saw just how massive it was. The front, or bow, was past us and heading into the open waters of the Gulf of Mexico; while the back, or stern of the ship, was still in the bay waters on the other side of the bridge.

David Phillip Parks

Above us, the massive steel cables supporting the bridge were in a series that went all the way up the tower, and glowed a soft orange from the lowering sun. Below us, we could see little people on the ship's upper deck walking around, looking up at us, or leaning against the railing enjoying the amazing views as they started their journey to the Caribbean Sea. As the ship headed westward, it looked like it was being guided by the setting sun.

We crossed over the ship and looked in both directions to appreciate how gigantic it was—it was like a majestic floating city! We saw several restaurants, swimming pools with many people splashing about, a jogging track with many runners and walkers on it, and even a basketball court with several games being played. There were many colorful umbrellas around the pools, and bright yellow lifeboats hanging off both sides of the lower decks. As the ship gracefully glided under us, the large smokestacks nearly touched the bottom of the bridge.

"Sometimes, these ships have to wait for low tide before they can go out to the Gulf because it's possible for them to be too high for the bridge's main span," Dad explained. "But the ship's captain knows the tide schedules, and knows when they can go through safely."

When the ship finally passed through, we could see the mighty thrust of the engines as the turbulent wake spread a wide bubbling trail of white water. It made waves that looked like colorful velvet with the rays of the sun glittering off the tops of each swell. Farther out in the Gulf, the water was so smooth, it looked like yellow-orange glass reflecting the brilliant sky above. As the ship moved out to sea, it passed small islands, dwarfing them. Soon, all we saw was its silhouette against the soft orange sky, and we hoped those people were having a wonderful time on their cruise.

Dad said, "Could you imagine being the captain of that ship?! You thought that airplane was big? You could put about 6 Boeing 737's on that ship—and 50 times the people … ya don't see THAT everyday back home, do ya kids!?" Then proudly added, "And you want power? That ship's engines have to move over 200,000 tons of steel, people, luggage, and food down to Aruba and back … like it's NOTH'IN!"

By the time we were thinking about all of that, we had driven the whole causeway over Tampa Bay and were back on land and heading south to Sarasota, and finally to Siesta Key. We were so glad to have seen the ship on the bay with the lowering sun, and hoped the light show continued in the sky as we continued heading south to our island.

Soon we saw 'Sarasota Next Right' on a sign and turned off the freeway, and headed west towards the Gulf and glowing reddish-orange sky. Mom and Dad wanted to drive through downtown Sarasota just to see it because they'd read about it many times in travel magazines. The city was beautifully tropical, and on its own bay. Then we followed the Siesta Key signs and went over a drawbridge, crossing Sarasota Bay with the city in the distance—it was incredible—we were almost there!

As we crossed over the drawbridge, we could see downtown Sarasota with a variety of sailboats anchoring for the night. We'd never seen a drawbridge before and Dad said they let bigger boats through by opening up, and are less expensive to build than the massive Sunshine Skyway crossing Tampa Bay.

Once we arrived on Siesta Key, we quickly found our condo building on the beach. It was just past sunset by the time we got our luggage up to our condo, so we just relaxed, and enjoyed the views of the amazing beach with the radiant sunset colors shimmering on the Gulf of Mexico.

David Phillip Parks 2018

Our condo was beautiful, with large windows allowing incredible views of the entire key, or island, and the long beach. The views from the 5th story were amazing in every direction.

So Mom said, "It's been a long day, lets unpack and go to a restaurant nearby for dinner … and then let's go for a walk on the beach!" We all thought that was a great idea, so after unpacking, we all freshened up and went out onto the balcony overlooking our little slice of paradise.

The humid evening air had a slight breeze, and we detected a comforting salty smell from the the Gulf's salt water and beach. I'd never smelled that before, and it seemed to clear our sinuses from the flight. Katie and I just looked around and said 'WOW' at the same time as Mom and Dad sweetly smiled, happy we made it there in good spirits and in good health.

We then walked down the stairs and met some other families in the parking area. Some were driving to go eat, some were riding bikes; while others were going for a walk on the beach or along Midnight Pass Road, where all the shopping, restaurants, and nightclubs were.

We heard some pleasant music from a live band in the distance, and Dad said it was from the Caribbean Islands called reggae. It was different than anything I'd ever heard before, and I really liked it! Dad started swaying his hips and arms to the music, making us laugh, and Mom laughed, "Phil, people are going to see you—quit it!"

He countered, "Hey … I'm just get'n warmed up!" as he loudly clapped his hands and spun around a few times, never missing a beat.

We decided to go to a famous fine dining restaurant just down the road called 'The Summerhouse Restaurant,' which was well known for its delicious food, atmosphere, and live entertainment. As we pulled into the entrance, the parking area was actually more like a beach within a jungle. There was a line of tourists waiting to get in, so we stopped and let a young man get in and drive our car away.

I was worried, "Dad, why'd you let that guy take our car away?!"

He chuckled, "David—he's the valet of this place—he's park'n the car for us—he'll bring it back to us later … get a GRIP!"

Mom jumped in, "Phil, he didn't know … don't be a jerk!"

"Who's a jerk? Your mother says don't be a jerk, Son!" as he nudged me into a plant as we walked along a path winding through the jungle.

"Alright, everybody behave," Mom warned when we got closer to the line.

The restaurant was partially hidden in the jungle, but as we made our way closer, it was unlike anything we'd ever seen before. The building was in an X shape that branched out into the jungle, and had a lobby in the middle. But the most striking features were the floor-to-ceiling glass walls, and the many tropical plants and small trees growing inside the restaurant. On the second floor there was a 'Tree Top' lounge where smooth jazz groups performed.

As night settled in, the lights were turned down, and colored lighting lit up the plants inside, and jungle outside, making for an unforgettable evening featuring the most delicious food on the Key. Only Mom brought some of her meal back to eat later at the condo. We really enjoyed our dinner, and the staff were all so friendly and professional.

Dad said, "Well … we're definitely come'n back here—no restaurants are like this back home … that's for sure!" We all happily agreed to that.

Before we headed back to the condo, we shopped for some groceries at a nice beach market right across the street from our building. Mom and Dad knew we needed food for breakfasts and lunches, but we planned on eating out for dinner every evening.

We ended the evening with a nice walk down the beach. There were many families taking in the view of the crescent moon near the horizon. It felt nice to walk in the warm Gulf waters gently lapping at our feet. We heard families speaking in German, Indian, Dutch, Spanish, Russian, Swedish, Italian, French, Portuguese, Mandarin, and Japanese. I'd never heard those languages before, so Mom explained which ones we were hearing.

Without lights nearby, the beach was very dark and many stars and constellations were visible—we even saw a shooting star! We noticed that many people stopped swimming after twilight set in, so I asked, "Why did all the people leave the water after sunset?"

Dad answered, "Well, you gotta be careful around now; sharks come in to feed near shore sometimes—some people stay in too long swimming and can get bit. But, many sharks here are nurse or lemon sharks, which are more docile. Kids, we gotta be careful of several things in the Gulf—sharks, jellyfish, barracuda, stingrays, and Portuguese man-of-wars can all be dangerous—stay away from them."

Katie got worried learning this, "Geez, is it any safer in the daytime to swim?!"

"Well sure it is, but you should learn some things before jumping in here … this isn't a lake in Ohio—this is part of the ocean, and we're entering their world. We need to be aware and respect the marine life here. We're not locals … we're not used to this, so we gotta learn some things. If we do dumb things, we could get seriously hurt or worse—so just be careful. Starting tomorrow, we'll be doing lots of swimming, so it's good to know something before we jump in—everybody understand?"

We nodded in understanding, "Yes Dad, we'll be careful."

"GOOD!" he shouted, jokingly, as he playfully kicked some water splashing Katie and me, making us run away laughing.

We stayed out on the beach for a few hours and even met a nice family from Argentina who were also staying at our condos. We were having such a nice time and so happy to be there with our new friends, we didn't want to go back to the unit. But, we'd had a big day, and started getting tired, so Mom and Dad said we should clean up and get some rest for a big day of fun tomorrow.

We said goodnight to the family, "We'll see you tomorrow!" They smiled and waved, "Hasta manana!" We were impressed with how they knew both English and Spanish.

Mom said, "That means, 'see you tomorrow.' When you two are older, you can learn a foreign language too—it's fun to learn new things!"

Katie and I shook our heads, and I thought, "Wow, that's so cool … another language!"

Katie smiled, "It sounds so nice … I can't wait to learn a new language soon!"

We headed up to the condo and went out onto the balcony for one last moment with the beach.

Mom shared what we were all thinking, "This place is magical!"

After brushing our teeth, we hugged Mom and Dad for bringing us down to paradise.

Dad yawned and rubbed his eyes, "Well, that's enough for me … time to hit the hay …" which was his way of saying he was going to bed.

Mom stayed up longer, and watched the Sarasota evening news. In about an hour, she turned off the lights and climbed into bed with Dad, who was already fast asleep.

One by one, all the tourists and locals alike went to sleep after another beautiful day on Siesta Key. As we slept, we dreamt of our new world of wonder: swimming with dolphins, building sand castles, laughing with new friends, and listening to reggae and smooth jazz, the soul of the Keys of Florida's Sun Coast.

After a good deep sleep, we all woke up early the next morning, and made some eggs, fruit, cereal, and yogurt for breakfast.

Mom then thought, "Hey, lets eat out on the lanai for a nice beach view!"

"That sounds great Honey, but what the heck's a 'lanai'?" Dad asked, confused. "Never heard that one before."

Katie and I were wondering too.

After Mom had her fun stumping us, she revealed, "I was reading a Florida magazine last night before bed, and lanais are a Hawaiian word for a side room; but in Florida, they use it for a porch, sunroom, or even balconies—it's fun learning something new!" she said, proudly.

Dad grabbed his food and headed to the large sliding glass doors overlooking the beach and Gulf, "Ok, see you on the sunroom-balcony-lanai-porch …"

We laughed and followed him to eat on the nice bamboo table and chairs. As we ate, we noticed the beach was getting crowded with early morning walkers, joggers, and bike riders. The air was cool this early, but was going to get hot and humid soon. Seagulls were soaring and crying out looking for food. Boats of different sizes were already out on the Gulf. The beach was long and curved slightly out farther north. Dad said it was called 'Crescent Beach' and was about 3.5 miles long, and we couldn't wait to explore all of it!

After eating, we stood at the railing and looked out, then down, and noticed our new friends were already at the beach; and their kids were busy building a sandcastle under a palm umbrella. And then, we saw 50 feet below, our own pool that we missed because it was surrounded by a dense area of palm trees, bushes, and flowers. We quickly got on our swimsuits, put some sunscreen on, grabbed a raft, beach towels, and ran down the stairs for a day of fun!

David Phillip Parks 2018

What happened next is something I'll never forget. Dad was so happy we were there, he decided to celebrate with the biggest cannonball splash on record. Dad was a big guy and powerfully built. He stood 5 ft. 11 inches tall, weighed 240 lbs., and was the strongest Dad I knew—he called it 'gorilla strength.' He was also the most playful, and when he was around a pool he always had to christen it with a water explosion—and that's just what he did.

He didn't care who was around, how close they were, or how much sunscreen they had on—he just put on a show of how to be fun. He playfully looked at Mom and nodded as if to say 'you know what's come'n!' She just shook her head, laughed, and sat in a chair with the Argentines—quickly moving out of the blast zone. With the intensity of a true pro, he ran full speed, jumped, and hit the calm water with a force that commands respect.

We saw unsuspecting tourists glance up at the last second, to hear … KA-BOOM!—followed by an explosion of spray. The wave from the blast rolled over our heads, and went over the pool sides. He came up from under the water smiling, seeing us laughing hysterically. He then noticed an older couple reading near the clubhouse who were soaked—reading glasses, books and all—and were in shock. But after seeing how hard children were laughing, they just grinned and nodded in understanding.

Dad glanced at them, "OOPS … sorry 'bout that!"

They appreciated why he did it and admitted in a British accent, "Very impressive, Sir! You actually cooled us off … we don't need to go swimming now—CHEERS!"

Dad then played with Katie and me, playfully throwing us around the pool. But we knew the Gulf of Mexico was waiting for us.

David Phillip Parker 2013

We splashed around in the pool for about a half hour, when Mom said, "Well, who's going to join me at the beach?"

The pool was fun, but there was so much more to do at the beach. We realized we hadn't been to the beach during the day yet, so we jumped out of the water, grabbed our stuff and followed her around the clubhouse. The Argentinian family said they'd meet us a little later.

We strolled down a little secluded beach area lined by wild sea grass and palm trees. The view of the Gulf through the palms was incredibly beautiful. The sky was the deepest blue, the water was a vibrant sea green, and the sand was almost blindingly white in the daytime. The sand's white color reflected the sun's energy, and wasn't hot to walk on. It was very fine and fluffy, and felt like soft baking powder under our feet. We also noticed how there were very few sea shells in the sand. Most other beaches we'd been to all had many hard shells that hurt to walk on, but Siesta's Crescent Beach had only a few small shells near the water.

We all walked together, and felt blessed to be in this tropical paradise. Everywhere we looked, something interesting was happening. In the water, people were sailing on a catamaran, kite boarding, wind surfing, boogie boarding, parasailing, and jet skiing. On the beach, some people were resting under umbrellas, others were playing football, soccer, baseball, volleyball, a paddle ball game called Kadima, or flying kites. But these kites were the professional type; they were large single or multiple colored kites of all designs that did advanced tricks over the beach, entertaining many families.

Once we were closer to water, we saw a family of dolphins swimming close together near the shore; it looked like they were interested in what people were doing, too. Swimmers were amazed at how close they were, as the dolphins gracefully glided by, like peaceful ambassadors of the sea.

David Phillip Parker

We got our beach towels spread out on the soft white sand. The harder, tanner sand near the water was almost like a street, with people using it to move along the 3 miles of beach. Most people liked walking, but many jogged or rode beach bikes; and a few even rode a hover board that had one wheel, which was ridden like a skateboard over the sand.

Katie decided to stay at her towel and talk to her Argentinian friends. Mom was enjoying a chat with a Swedish family next to her, while Dad went for a swim and to look for seashells, so I went with him. But we spent most of the time wrestling in the water; and I got worn out trying to move him as he laughed while dunking or throwing me. So after I got enough salty Gulf water in my mouth and eyes, I needed to take a break.

"Have you had enough, Son? … or do you need another WATER WHOOP'N!?"

I decided to give it one more try and jumped him, then got lifted over his head and thrown upside down about seven feet away. I popped up to hear him laugh, "YOU'LL LEARN— you don't mess with a SILVERBACK GORILLA!"

"Hey Dad, I'm gonna walk down to that point over there … I think it's called the 'Point of Rocks'—I'll be back for more, later!"

"Ok, we'll be have'n lunch around 1, so if you wanna eat, get back around then."

"Alright, I will—see ya, Dad!"

It was starting to get warm; 85 degrees before noon was something I wasn't used to during summer in Ohio. So I walked in the shallow water pools, and I really liked how the breaking waves washed over my feet—that felt really good! I couldn't believe all the different things people were doing around me in the water: a family was building an amazing sandcastle, a couple were paddle boarding, a boy and girl were boogie boarding near shore, some people were snorkeling, and a few people farther out were scuba diving near an under-water reef, while others were on a big

David Phillip Parka

catamaran headed out to the deep water. As I got closer to the point, I noticed people fishing out in the water, and wondered what they were catching. I was sure the fish here were very different than what I was used to back home.

When I was finally down near the Point of Rocks, I realized why it had that name; there were many large flat rocks and coral reefs that stuck up out of the water. It seemed like a nice place to rest, look for shells, snorkel, or fish from the concrete breakwall that had colorful graffiti art on it. There were nice beach houses in this area near the shore, and I thought how lucky these people were to live here, with the Gulf of Mexico as their backyard!

As I came up on the large breakwall, I noticed a wading bird that was very thin and having trouble walking in the shallow surf. I looked hard through the clear water, and saw the bird had a serious injury to its right leg. A plastic fishing line was wrapped around its lower leg and had severed most of the foot off; only a tiny piece of tendon held the foot to the leg. The foot was floating behind the hobbling bird, being dragged along with each step.

Then I remembered the bird was an egret. It was trying hard to get some fish to eat, but its injury made it impossible for it to lunge its beak into the water fast enough to catch the darting little fish around it. I worried the bird would soon starve to death, and I felt sad that such a beautiful bird could die this way. I followed it to the wall and tried to get closer, but when I got a few feet away, it flapped its wings, caught the breeze, and flew away to the other side of the reef.

I thought I needed to try to help it, so I climbed the wall and made my way around to a cove on the other side of the wall. There I saw the egret had landed in the shallow end of the cove; maybe I could get to it and try to grab it. But a large barrier of reef boulders separated me from the cove, so I started climbing them.

David Phillip Park

On the far end of the small cove, a group of girls noticed the injured bird and began walking towards it. I kept my eye on the bird, but I was having a challenge getting over the boulders because they had many sharp edges that hurt my feet, so I had to go slower than I wanted. The waves were bigger on this end of the beach, and broke over the rocks with big splashes, wetting me each time.

The egret was getting closer to the girls, and as I made my way carefully down to the water, they looked at me with concern in their eyes; they were worried about the egret too. I walked up to them, "That bird is hurt … it needs help."

They watched it carefully and the blonde girl spoke first, "We noticed that too—it's very thin."

The girl next to her added, "Is there something wrong with its leg? It's having trouble walking … poor thing!"

The third girl said, firmly, "We should try to help it!"

Keeping my eye on the bird, I said, "That's why I followed it over here, I'm trying to get close enough to grab it. Is there a place around here that could help it?"

The girls looked at each other, "Yeah, there's the Mote Marine Laboratory in Sarasota," the blonde girl said, intensely.

I thought we should do something fast before it flew away, "Ok, lets try something before it gets away!"

David Phillip Parker

The girls agreed, with the blonde one saying quickly, "Alright, let's surround it and jump in—we're only gonna get one chance at this—it's gonna get scared and try to fly away."

The girl in white said, "We gotta be fast but gentle—we don't want to hurt it more than it already is!"

The girl in red said, "Ok … let's do this!"

We all moved into position around it, keeping a little distance so that it didn't get too nervous. Once we were in position, we all looked at each other, nodded in agreement, then faced the bird, which was already on alert and looking at us all around it.

As we all opened our arms, the blonde girl took a deep breath, locked her focus on the egret, and firmly said, "NOW!"

In an instant, we all lunged toward the egret and reached out to grab it. The egret cried out loudly in distress and jumped in panic, flapping as hard as it could, and lifted out of the water. As we reached it, we all frantically grabbed at it, but its wings flapped furiously; and with all its remaining strength, it escaped our grasping hands, and soared out of the surf and into the air, to safety and freedom.

David Phillip Ra

We watched it lift higher above the outer cove, and gracefully soar into the deep, distant blue sky.

We were all disappointed, when the girl in white, frustrated, blurted out, "GEEZ! If we only had a blanket to throw over it—we could've gotten it!"

The girl in red added, "Poor thing, it needs to eat soon, or it won't last long …"

The blonde girl was disappointed, "We did the best we could guys … say a prayer for it …"

We all silently watched it fly away, and shared a sense of sadness. Once it was out of sight, we all sort of sighed and the girls looked at each other, and then at me. By their reaction, I could sort of sense they weren't tourists, and might be locals.

The blonde girl looked at me intently, "Did you see the fishing line hanging off its leg when it was flying away?"

"Yeah, I saw that over there on the other side of the wall, and followed it over here. The line cut into its leg … its right foot was cut off and dangling behind it as it tried to walk," I said, sadly.

She said, "Well, we've seen that before—what a shame! I just hate when something so beautiful suffers because of our ignorance!"

The girl in white lowered her head with a frown and shook her head in disgust, "We know … it happens all the time to many of the birds and fish … even the larger species are affected, like dolphins and manatees. It's a big problem down here."

The blonde girl said with resolution, "Well, we're going to do something—we'll report this to the Mote Marine!"

Then she noticed my disappointment, and wanted to reassure me that what we tried, successful or not, was the right thing to do, "You care about nature, don't you?"

I was looking down and nodded, "Yeah, I care a lot. We live with a lot of nature back home; I was really hoping we could help that bird." She stepped toward me, and said something that changed me, and something I'll never forget.

"It's nice to see you care, many people don't—that's too bad for them. That egret lived a wonderful life—we're lucky to have it in our world each day. Don't worry for it … that bird's soul has been here many times before, and it will live on again in countless forms forever—each time getting better. Its end will be its beginning … do you understand?"

I didn't know what to say. I'd never heard someone her age say something like that, but it made sense to me. All I could do was nod.

"You're not from around here, are you?" she said curiously. "What's your name?"

"I'm Dave. I'm not from here, I'm from Ohio."

"Well, I'm Jay, that's Jen, and that's Ashley … nice to meet you."

"It's nice to meet you too," I awkwardly responded, feeling the focused gaze of the older girls.

Sensing my shyness, Jay said, eagerly, "Ohio, wow, we've never been up north … isn't it really cold there?" Then jokingly said with a grin, "Aren't there glaciers and polar bears in your yard?!"

David Phillip Pa

She put me at ease and I knew she was joking with me, "Yeah, it gets real cold in winter, but I haven't seen any glaciers, or polar bears in our yard yet—I'll keep look'n though!" I tried to joke back. Jay smiled at my attempt to be witty, but Jen and Ashley just sort of smirked. Then I asked "Are you from here?"

"Yeah, we live down here. We've never seen snow, or ice. The coldest it's been here is maybe 50—that's freezing to us!"

I laughed at that, "50 … that's a heatwave for Ohio winters—we've seen it go to 20 below zero—and 30 below wind chills—and 2 feet of snow in big blizzards."

I felt more relaxed with them and comfortable, and we walked towards each other, with Jen now smiling, "30 below … that's CRAZY COLD—I couldn't handle that! What do you do when it's that cold?!"

"Well, when it's that cold, it's deadly. We don't go anywhere and stock up on food and stuff. It usually lasts a few days, then it'll go back above zero—that's normal for us. But, we have a blast in winter—it's fun!"

"Fun? How's it fun trying not to get frostbite?!" Jay said joking again, but very interested.

"Oh, we do all kinds of stuff—we're lucky to have all four seasons. It depends on the kind of cold we get."

Jay became very curious, "The 'kind' of cold? Isn't cold just cold?" as Jen nodded and laughed.

Then I explained in better detail what my world up north was like. As I began, I noticed that Jay and Jen were both very interested, but not so for Ashley, who seemed to look down, not wanting to spend more time with a kid from up north on a beautiful sunny day.

DavidPhillipP

"Back home, Ohio turns into a winter wonderland. The 'kind' of cold we get decides what we do for fun. If it's just cold, we'll go ice skating and play hockey on a pond, but if it's cold with lots of snow, we'll go sled riding. Some older kids even go skiing."

Jay and Jen imagined a world they'd never experienced, "It sounds fun, Dave—tell us what it's like!"

So I took them back to my world, over 1,100 miles away. "Well, we're near Lake Erie, it's only an hour away, and from December until early April, there's usually snow on the ground. We usually get about 6 inches each snowfall all winter long, but some years big blizzards come off the lake and we get buried—like 2 feet! My dad and I have to go up on the roof and shovel the snow off, or its heavy weight will damage the roof. Then we have to shovel the driveway, or we can't go anywhere."

"WOW, I can't imagine that—and this can go on all winter long?!" Jen asked, in disbelief.

"Well, it could, but most winters the snow will melt back some—we're used to it."

Then Jay seemed concerned, "If it snows that much and can be that cold, how can someone have fun in those conditions—isn't it too dangerous with frostbite?"

"It gets dangerous when it's below zero—we don't go outside then—my mom and dad won't let us. But, the schools all close for a day or two, and we get a winter vacation. So if it's above zero, all the kids get together in the morning, and we go sled riding all day at the hills behind our house, back in the farm and in the woods—it's a blast!"

Then Ashley seemed to be getting curious about winter fun, "Well, how many kids go?"

"There's a lot of kids just on our street—maybe 15 around my age, and we'll meet up with more kids from other streets at the hills. The older kids get there first and make the runs with their big inner tubes. By the time we get there, the fluffy snow is all packed down and the runs get really fast!"

"Does everybody use inner tubes?" Jen wondered.

"No, the younger kids use sleds—they're faster than the tubes, and you can steer 'em."

"Why don't the older kids use sleds? Are sleds too small for them?" Ashley wondered.

"The older kids can be high schoolers, and they like to jump on the tubes in groups and go down all together—or they'll tie their tubes together and go down in a big gang of people … but they usually go to the huge hills for that—we just go to the smaller hills close to our house."

"How fast can you go on the smaller hills?" Jay asked, smiling.

"We can go as fast as a bike on the street. The main hill's called Niagara. It's got a small stream at the bottom, which makes every run scary, 'cuz you gotta stop your sled fast, or you're go'n in!" I said, laughing. "You can't screw around on Niagara Hill—you gotta know what you're do'n or you'll be go'n home real fast soaking wet! A girl on the next street did that … we warned her if she went too fast to just jump off and let the sled go."

"Oh my God … this is too funny!" Ashley laughed, "So what happened to her … she got soaked, didn't she?!"

"Yep, she sure did! She held on, jumped the bank, and flew face first into the middle of the stream and rode her sled underwater … it looked like someth'n out of a funny movie!"

Jen was laughing, "That's unreal!"

The girls were all wide eyed imagining all this, "I've never thought about sled riding living down here—it's so different than anything we're used to—but that was a good story! I feel bad for that girl, though," Jay admitted, smiling.

"Wow—I wish we could go sled riding and inner tubing … it sounds so FUN!" Jen said, laughing.

Then I wondered what they did during the winter months, "So what's your winter like down here in Florida?"

"Well, we have lots of fun too, but it's on the water," Jay said, excitedly.

Then Ashley jumped in, "Yeah, and instead of sleds, we use surfboards!"

"Wow—that sounds really fun! What's surfing like? I've only seen it on TV."

Then the girls brought me into their world, and Jay happily described when they do it, "Well, the Gulf is usually pretty calm most of the year, but it gets really windy in the winter months, and the waves kick up then. That's when we do most of our surfing—from December through April."

"But that's when the rip currents can get strong, so we gotta be careful not to get caught in them," Jen said.

"What happens in a rip current?" I wondered.

"Well, they happen year round down here," Ashley explained, "but they're stronger in the winter months, with the bigger waves. They can quickly carry a swimmer down the beach, and then out to the deep water far from shore. They're dangerous, so we study the water before we go in, and we look out for each other."

Then Jen added, "We all learned to surf when we were little—younger than you! So we've been doing it for a long time. It feels like you're flying over the water—it's amazing! It's our favorite thing to do!" they smiled and all nodded in agreement.

David Phillip Park

"If you've ever been skateboarding, it's kind'a like that—just standing on a bigger board though. But there's several kinds of surfing: short and long board, and paddle-in or tow-in. Pros use everything, but they'll use short boards for tricks and shredding inside the barrel or on top of the wave; longboards are used for long straight rides. Paddle-in is what we do—just paddling into and catching a wave, whereas tow-in is for the big waves—a jet ski or wave runner is used to quickly pull a surfer into waves that are too big and fast to paddle into."

"Wow—that's so cool! What's the biggest waves you've ever surfed?!" I asked, amazed.

Jay laughed, "Well Dave, we surf for fun, so we paddle-in and have a great time—nothing stressful—we usually don't surf anything over ten feet … that's good enough for us!"

"Yeah, we do it to relax and get a rush all at the same time, but big wave riders do it to compete for prize money all over the world; and the waves they tow into can get over 70 feet—imagine a seven story building coming down on you! Each year, some surfers drown when they can't handle the size or speed of monster waves," Ashley said, seriously.

"That's not what surfing's about for us—we're soul surfers—it's about connecting with the ocean's power and beauty," Jen said, smiling.

"We try to ride through the barrel if the wave is bigger than us; if it's not, we just ride down the face of it. Or sometimes we'll surf up on top of the wave as it's breaking and ride down the break water in front of the wave … we can ride them to shore sometimes. Once you become a strong swimmer, you should try surfing someday, Dave, you'd love it!" Jen said, smiling, confidently.

"I think I will someday—I'll need to practice first, then I'll go surfing with you!" I teased, and we all laughed.

David Phillip Pan

They seemed to really be interested in my life in Ohio, "So, when it's not winter, what do you do back home?" Jen wondered.

"Well, when winter's over, and spring comes, we like ride'n our bikes, especially in the fields. We made really good trails and all the kids use them to get all around the outside of our town. We even have trails going through the woods all around our area; and they connect with the ones in the fields—we use'em like roads."

"That's smart—it's a good way to avoid car traffic on the streets," Jay thought.

"On some trails, there's giant dirt mounds, and we ride over 'em as fast as we can so we get a good jump over the other side. My buddies will do someth'n funny like kick their legs out and yell or honk at the top of the jump!"

"No way … that's funny! Sounds like you guys are serious bikers!" Jen said. "You have good bikes?"

"Yeah, ride'n bikes is a blast! Our bikes are good enough—but we beat'em up a lot, so we don't have expensive stuff. Good enough to get around and get muddy! How 'bout you, do you all bike down here?"

David Phillip Panko 2019

Jay's eyes got big as she smiled, "Yeah, we bike almost everyday! Our bikes are a little different from your bikes though. We ride beach bikes—they're bigger and heavier, and have wide tires for the fluffy sand and water."

"We ride our bikes throughout the day to get around too, but our favorite time to ride is during sunset—it's absolutely beautiful riding along the water as the sky turns so many pretty colors!" Jen said.

"Don't you get wet doing that?" I wondered.

"OH YEAH … that's the point!" Ashley laughed. "But we're wearing our bathing suits—it's really fun splashing through the water!"

"Yeah, our sunsets are famous on Siesta Beach," Jen said, proudly. "We like riding by all the tourists. If it's really warm, we'll park the bikes, and go for a quick swim. To see all the colors in the sky reflect off the water is unbelievable!"

"And that's when families of dolphins come in to feed near shore. They're so smart and cute—they can come right up to shore!" Ashley grinned. "But riding bikes here can be a challenge during high season around Thanksgiving through Easter."

"Why, what happens?" I wondered.

"Well, there's so many people on the beach then—we have to be careful. Sometimes it's so crowded, we have to get off and walk our bikes. That's fun too, because we can meet tourists," Jen admitted.

"It's fun riding along the shore; but the saltwater isn't good for the bikes, so we always wash them afterwards—they'd get all rusty if we didn't," Jay explained. "No matter how many times we ride the beach, it always feels new; to see the sailboats on the Gulf with the sunset, it's just magical!"

"And like you said Dave, we can get anywhere on our bikes. Like when the drawbridges are up, we can get to places faster than cars can, because they're all stuck in traffic jams!" Jen said, smiling.

Then Ashley wondered, "So, what's your autumn season like back in Ohio?"

"Well, the weather gets cooler and the leaves all change different colors. Our Japanese maples turn bright red, the maples turn orange or yellow, the hickories turn gold, the elms turn yellow, the oaks turn brown or redish brown."

Jay smiled, "Oh, I would love to see that—all those colors—you're so lucky!"

"But they fall to the ground in a few weeks and turn the ground all those colors—and then we rake'em into big piles that are taller than you."

"Why do that … isn't that a lot of work?" Ashley asked.

"It's not all work—we play in them first! My dad rakes'em into huge piles, and all the kids climb our big maple tree and jump off the branches into the leaves. My buddy Jerry usually jumps first 'cuz he's the leaf tester, and sees if the pile is high enough for jumping—it's really fun!"

"I would love that—I wish we could do that down here!" Jen laughed.

"Well, once we jump into them enough, the piles get all smashed down, and then we all get into a big leaf fight, wrestle and throw each other all around—it's super fun! My dad just laughs at us! Then we rake'em into big sheets, and carry'em into the field. Then I wrestle my dad in them, but he's so strong, he just throws me all over the place—I eat a lot'a leaves!" I laughed.

"Wow, we can't do anything like that down here—you guys have a lot of good 'old fashion fun,' don't you?!" Jay realized.

"Yeah, we sure do! I'd miss not do'n that down here," I said, wistfully.

"Well, we climb into trees too! Sometimes on nice days, we'll take our paddle boards and kayak and go across Sarasota Bay to some small islands for a tropical picnic," Jay said.

"Why would you climb trees for a picnic?" I asked, confused.

"Our picnics are a little different—it can be dangerous in some areas near the water because of crocodile or alligators, so we just string a hammock high up between two trees, and have a nice time enjoying the city over the bay."

"Are crocodiles and alligators everywhere down here?" I asked, concerned.

"They're mostly in certain areas at the water's edge, but they usually sleep in the day, and feed at night. We're pretty safe being up in a hammock, but we wouldn't do that at night, though," Jay said, seriously.

"It's so nice to get away from everything out on the islands," Jen explained. "There's trails on them to walk around. About late fall for us, our trees lose some leaves too, and go into dormancy. It's like a resting period, but they don't change colors. These islands are like little tropical parks with lots of things to explore. Nobody lives on them, and that's what we like—just peace and quiet—no cell phone chatter and noise … we can't stand all that!"

"Wow, that sounds really fun … I'd like to explore those islands too—when I'm older!" I admitted, making the girls smile.

David Phillip

"So what do you like to do in summer?" Ashley asked.

"We do a lot of different stuff. Our summers are usually in the mid 80s to low 90s, but it can get hot … as hot as Florida, but not as humid. It can go to 100 degrees during heat waves, so we go swimming a lot, or to a Lake Erie beach. One thing I like to do is go on my zip line through our backyard; it goes all the way from our house down to a farmer's field. On warm days, it feels good flying through the shaded woods."

"We have zip lines down here too, some go through jungles, others will go over a beach, and some go over water too," Jay said. "But many of them you have to pay to ride on, but you get nice long rides."

"Well, my zip line goes over some water … my little stream that flows along our woods into the farmer's field. It's a shorter line, maybe 100 feet long, so nobody's gonna pay me to ride it, but it's fine for me!" I said with a big smile.

Ashley added, "Yeah, but we don't have zip lines in our backyards … that would be pretty cool if we did! How fast does yours go?"

"Ours starts about 30 feet up in a maple tree, and it goes pretty fast. By the time it gets to the stream, it's go'n about as fast as I can run. Plus, it can spin around, so I can go backwards or sideways on it. But it's cool how it feels like I'm flying through the woods like a bird. Our yard is like a park; we have big owls, hawks, and wood peckers that live in the big old trees, plus lots of smaller birds like cardinals, blue jays, robins, and finches. There's also lots of squirrels, chip monks, raccoons, and deer in the woods."

"Wow, your yard sounds very peaceful and quiet. I bet all those animals see you flying through the woods, too!" Jay laughed.

"Hey, we go flying too, but instead of a zip line, we're being pulled by a speed boat!" Jen said, excitedly.

"Oh, I just saw that down here today, you mean when you're up on that parachute thing that goes over the water?"

"Yep—it's called 'parasailing'—it's really popular down here."

"Isn't that kind'a scary? I saw it go up really high—like way higher than the taller buildings around here."

"It's a little scary at first, but once you get used to it, it's amazing! We all go together and get strapped into a harness. The big parachute is attached to the harness, and it's all pulled by the boat. You start on the back of the boat, and as the boat picks up speed, the chute starts to lift us up," Jen explained.

"How high does it go?"

"It depends—some people don't want to go too high, while others like to go up to the limit of 500 feet, and about 800 feet of line."

"Which way do you like, low or high?"

"We like both—we go all the way up first—we can see Tampa from that height and that's like 60 miles away; then, when we're coming back down to the boat, we like to go down to the water and drag our feet through it—it feels really good on a hot day!"

"Yeah, it's so exciting to soar over Siesta Key! We can see everybody on the beach, all the roads and buildings, and the Intra-Coastal that separates the Keys from the mainland. It's breathtakingly beautiful up there!" Jay said, beaming.

"You should try it before you go back home, Dave!" Ashley said, with a big smile.

"It looks amazing to do!" I said, nodding.

"It's summer in Ohio now, so what else do you do up there?" Jen wondered.

"Well, we do all kinds of things; it depends on the weather. If it's hot, we'll go swimming at a big public pool, but most days we just play sports—usually football, basketball or baseball. Sometimes I'll play catch with my dad after work, or play tennis with my mom and sister. At night, all the kids will play ghost in the graveyard, or flashlight tag—we're always do'n something. We only go inside to eat supper. My mom makes delicious family meals and we all talk, then we'll go watch something good on TV."

"With all those sports you play, which one is your favorite?" Jay asked.

"I think football is our favorite sport. We play that all year long, even in the snow. We have the Cleveland Browns and Pittsburgh Steelers teams near us, and the Ohio State Buckeyes. Basketball's our next favorite; the Cleveland Cavaliers won the NBA Championship a few years ago! We also play baseball sometimes on the street. We have the Cleveland Indians and Pittsburgh Pirates to root for—sports are a big deal in our area," I explained. "What sports do you play down here?"

David Phillips

"People play all those sports here, too," Jay said. "For football we root for the Tampa Bay Buccaneers, for basketball, we have the Orlando Magic and the Miami Heat. For baseball, we have the Tampa Bay Rays. But the sport the three of us play the most here is beach volleyball—it's a lot of fun in the sand and a great workout. Then we go for a swim after to wash all the sand off, so it's kind'a like two sports together," making Jen and Ashley laugh in agreement.

"Beach volleyball is very competitive here; we have serious matches all the time. And at the public beach, we can even watch semi-pro or pro matches. Players from all over the world play here—it's really exciting to see! And there's several ways to play: some people play 6 on 6, some do 4 on 4, 3 on 3, but the hardest is 2 on 2."

Then Jen added, "Because it's warm down here for most of the year, people can play most sports year round. It's interesting meeting people from around the world—it's easy to do playing beach volleyball."

"I've played that a few times—it's fun, but I'm no pro!" I joked. "What countries do the other players come from?"

"Oh, we've played with people from all over, but I'd say most come from South America—many are from Brazil and Argentina, and they're excellent soccer players, too. In fact, we've seen some South Americans play beach volleyball with their feet only—no hands … can you believe that?!" Ashley asked, challengingly, as I just shook my head in disbelief.

David Phillip Pank

Then I wondered, "How do you spend the holidays—what's it like without snow around Christmas and New Years?"

"Well, we kinda do the same things you do up north, just a little differently," said Jen. "We decorate Christmas trees, but here some people use seashells for ornaments—it's Christmas Siesta Key style!"

"Do kids get time off from school? We get a 2-3 week Christmas break, and even when we do have school, the blizzards can get so bad, schools cancel classes and we get to stay home."

"We get a 2 week break around Christmas," Ashley said.

"Do you stay inside during really bad snowstorms?" Jay asked.

"Heck no … we go outside and always get in snowball fights with all the neighbor kids! When the snow is deep enough, we build huge snow forts, then dig tunnels into them. Sometimes the tunnels get so big, they're like small rooms that everyone can fit into," I explained, proudly.

"How long do the snowball fights last? Is there ever a winner?" Jay asked, laughing.

"They'll go on for hours! It takes a while to build the snow forts, then everybody makes snowballs, then we blast each other with everything we got!"

"What about cars or trucks going by?" Ashley wondered.

"We stop throwing to let them go by, but once they're past, we all let loose again and blast each other until our arms get tired—it's awesome! Usually someone's mom makes hot chocolate and cookies after we're done—it tastes great after a big battle!" I said, smiling. "I guess the only time there's a real winner is when someone's fort falls down and there's nowhere to hide!" which made the girls smile and shake their heads in disbelief. "So, do you do anything special during the holiday season?"

David Phillip Pa

"Well, we certainly don't get into snowball fights—but that does sound really fun … I want to get in a snowball fight now!" Jen laughed.

"Yeah, me too, but we'll never have snow down here," Ashley said, disappointed.

"Yeah, we don't have snow, but we have lots of sand! And, our sand is some of the best in the world—we win competitions for best sand, and we've won best beach awards in the U.S!" Jay said, proudly.

"Instead of making snow forts, we can pack our sand and make sand sculptures. Some years when the weather is good, Siesta Key holds professional sand sculpting competitions during the holiday season. Siesta Beach is our main public beach, and it holds the sculpting competition. Pros from around the world come here and they'll create anything you can imagine—from sorcerers, to the Statue of Liberty, mermaids, dragons, sea turtles—anything! And the sand's so white and fluffy, it looks just like snow!" Ashley said, happily.

"How big do the sculptures get?" I wondered.

"They can get HUGE—I mean, like bigger than a car!" Jen said throwing her arms out wide. "Front end loaders have to push the sand into big mounds, then the sculptors get their tools and spend all day shoveling, digging, scrapping, packing and patting down their creations—it's incredible what they do! Thousands of people come to see the sand sculptures!"

"Wow, it sounds so cool! I've built lots of sandcastles, but they just look like a big lump, and then they just kind'a fall over!" I joked, making the girls laugh. "My family would really like to see that sand sculpture competition!"

David Phillip Pan

"Water's such a big part of our lives down here. Does your family do any kind of boating for fun?" Jay asked.

"Well, we've gone on sightseeing cruises around Cleveland, and we also have friends who have a speed boat—they go waterskiing a lot. They take us waterskiing too—I'm just learning though. Our friends go to a big river near us in western Pennsylvania, on the Allegheny River. My buddy Brian taught me how to do it—he's really good! My mom, dad, and sister can all ski, too. The river is nice to be on. It's in the foothills of the Allegheny Mountains, so it's hilly there, and the river flows down to Pittsburgh—it's a really fun time going there!"

"That's impressive, Dave—your whole family does it, that's pretty cool!" Ashley said, as Jay and Jen nodded.

I explained, "My dad had a speed boat before he met my mom—they actually met on a waterskiing date. My dad's a great skier—he can do it on one ski!"

"That's called slaloming," Jay helped me.

"Yeah—he can slalom and goes all over behind the boat—it's so cool … I hope to do that too, someday!"

"You will if you keep practicing Dave, don't give up!" Jen said, encouragingly. "It's nice your whole family does that with your friends. We all ski with our friends, too; some have boats, others use wave runners."

"Wow, I don't know anyone who has a wave runner—they're really fast, right?" I wondered.

David Phillip Perk

"Yep, they're pretty fast! Ours goes 50 mph—that's good enough for us, but some can easily go over 70," Jen said. "They're nice to have. We can go anywhere quickly, and we don't need a big trailer to move it, or store it at a marina slip—we just keep it at our house."

"We like to jump on it and go see someplace we've never seen before. My favorite places to check out are the many mangrove forests," Ashley said.

"What are mangrove forests?" I wondered.

"They're beautiful groups of trees and shrubs that live in coastal intertidal zones—where salt water from the Gulf meets with fresh water from land. They can grow together and make dense forests that grow over your head, while you paddle through them on a network of waterways. They are known for amazing root systems that grow into the water, and many times there's coral reefs around them," Jay said.

"We often bring our snorkeling or scuba gear, and go for dives to check out the underwater reefs, and mangrove roots for all the marine life that live there. We see many colorful fish, crabs, and even dolphins go there. We try to keep these tidal regions clean by removing trash or litter. We'll report conditions or problems of these eco systems to our local oceanographers, and marine biologists. If the mangroves and coral are healthy, then we're healthy … we're all connected to each other in nature, Dave."

"My mom and dad teach us that, too. I'm glad you do that down here; I'm gonna tell my parents, and even my science teacher, what you do. I think more people should do that!" Then I thought, "Well, Florida seems beautiful all the time, but what's it like when the weather gets stormy?"

"Usually we can get an afternoon rain storm, which feels nice because it cools us down. But they don't last long, maybe an hour, then they clear up or move on," Jen said.

David Phillip Parks

"But I'm sure you know we get hurricanes too, don't you?" Jay asked.

"Yeah, my mom and dad teach us about those, and we learn about them in science class at school, too."

"That's good—it's important to understand them, and how they affect this region. Florida's west coast has had many hurricanes go by as weaker storms—Category 1 or 2; but, it hasn't had a direct hit by a major storm—like a Cat 4 or 5. So even though the hurricanes were smaller and less intense, we've gotten serious flooding and some wind damage. Near the coast, big waves and strong rip currents and tides are very dangerous, so police work with the Coast Guard to keep people off the beaches and water when storms are approaching. Usually, we have time to take shelter, or leave the area if we want."

Jen said firmly, "We're prepared for smaller storms that we don't evacuate for by having lots of food, blankets, water, a generator, flashlights, candles, matches, a radio, things like that in case the power is out for a while. If the storms get big and we have to evacuate, we'd leave early to avoid traffic jams; which is a serious problem since so many people live on Florida's coasts. But since the oceans are warming, some hurricanes have been weaker one day, and then explode in strength to Cat 4 or 5, catching everyone off guard, so it's harder to evacuate when people are panicking and trying to leave all at the same time—especially with the limited number of bridges going over to all the Keys—that's a serious problem down here."

"We pray we never get hit by a major storm, because a Cat 5 can have winds of 157+ and gusts can go over 200mph. Storms like that completely destroy large coastal regions, and flood entire states at a time," Jay said, seriously. "Hurricanes are an important part of nature; they help balance the energy in the atmosphere and oceans on a giant scale."

Then I wondered, "Why do so many people risk everything by living in the tropics then? Isn't there a better way to live down here, knowing these storms come each year?"

"Those are good questions. People love the warm weather year round down here, so they're hoping the storms miss their locations; but, it's a gamble to be on the coasts, or mainland. Sooner or later, a hurricane's gonna hit, they can't be stopped. We can live in a safer way with them by making developers build one story off the ground—up on stilts or piles, or risers. These lift a house or building up maybe 12 feet so flood water can pass through without damaging the structure. In these regions, it's much better to build this way," Jen said.

"Geez, you have to be pretty tough to live down here. I didn't know all that … it's a lot to think about, isn't it?" I thought.

"Yeah, it's a lot to deal with when they hit, but most of the time it's beautiful here, so we've been lucky. But we're prepared and aware of the risks—it's just normal life in paradise!" Ashley said, shrugging her shoulders and grinning.

"Hey, we're not the only tough ones though; we know you guys get some bad weather too in the summer … what's that like?" Jay asked.

"We sure do! Ohio's on the outer edge of 'Tornado Alley' that runs across the plain states and midwest. We get tornadoes every year too, and so far, our town hasn't been hit yet … but they've hit all around our area."

"That sounds scary to us! We get small tornadoes from hurricanes, or isolated waterspouts, but they're not powerful. Tell us more about your big storms; aren't you afraid to live with them?!" Jen said, shaking her head.

"Yeah, it's scary when the big storms come with the squall lines. But most of them don't make tornadoes, just really high winds, hail, booming lightning and flash floods. It's actually kind'a amazing to watch those storms go through. I like sitting on the front porch with my dad and watch all the lightning and hear the thunder explode over our heads—it's exciting! But when the storms get too big, our town's tornado siren goes off, letting us know there's a tornado nearby, or conditions that can make one. We'll watch the weather radar alerts on TV, and when the trees are really blowing around, or the electricity goes out, we know it's time to head down to the basement underground. We're prepared too with blankets, a radio, snacks, and water."

"Have you ever seen one? That would be incredible to see!" Jay thought.

"Well, I've seen about 10 funnel clouds, before they go all the way down to the ground. But, if we're at home, we're always in the basement, and my sister and I hide under our heavy pool table—we only do that when it sounds like a jet engine outside. We can't see anything down there, but we sure hear it roaring!"

"Oh my God, I don't know if I could handle all that!" Jen said, with big eyes.

David Phillips

"Yeah, my dad works for a telecommunications company, and he puts in the phones, wires and sometimes telephone poles for our city, and one year part of our city got destroyed by the biggest tornado in our states' history—it was an F5—that's the biggest tornadoes get."

"How powerful is that compared to a big hurricane? Because like Jen just said, we get tornadoes too," Ashley asked, concerned.

"Well, tornadoes don't last long like hurricanes do, and since they're smaller, they don't affect huge areas like hurricanes do. But, I learned the winds in a F5 or EF5 can be over 200—and some can be over 300mph!"

"How can anything survive that!?" Jay asked, astonished.

"Well, nothing can … even the strongest buildings are destroyed or just blown away. There's nothing left when those types of tornadoes go through. They even remove roads, sections of parking lots … houses and some buildings can just explode and get carried away," I said, seriously.

"That's horrible! How often does this happen in your area?!" Ashley asked, shocked.

"Only three F5's have hit our state. Usually, our county gets several small tornadoes a season, and other years we can get more—each year is different. But our region is very industrial, so we have damage that isn't common in other parts of the country that get tornadoes. We have many steel mills and heavy industry, so when that gets destroyed, that's a really powerful tornado. But, most of our tornadoes are between F0 and F3—they happen every summer—it's just something we have to live with. But I'm really interested in them. And like you said, we can't stop 'em, we just gotta build things better. Each tornado is different. F0's and 1's are thin like ropes, and they grow in size, so an F5 or EF5 can be over 2 miles wide, and be on the ground for 50-100 miles, or more. F0's to F2's blow things down, F3's to F4's blow things away, and F5's blow things apart—like explosive power."

DavidPhillipParker

"Like we said before, you guys are tough up there in Ohio—you got blizzards, ice storms, below zero, flash floods, hail, lightning, 100 degrees, tornadoes … anything else?!" Ashley asked, sarcastically.

I thought for a moment, "Yeah … we can get earthquakes too—our area had a 4.0 magnitude on the Richter Scale—I almost bounced out'a bed!"

"Well I don't know if you saw on your news, but we also have to deal with something called the Red Tide—have you heard about it?" Jay asked.

"I saw something on the news about it—is it in the water and hurts the fish?" I thought. "That's about all I know."

"Yeah, it's a microscopic algae bloom that turns the water a reddish brown and it kills marine life from shellfish and clams up to dolphins, manatees, sharks, sting rays and turtles—it's horrible! Ashley said, sadly.

"And, it releases spores into the air that are harmful to breathe. It makes you choke and beaches are littered with dead marine life of all kinds … and they just decay on the shore, making it smell awful! It's so sad to see so many beautiful creatures die that way!"

"And most of it is caused by humans; we pollute the water with too many fertilizers and farm run off and the algae just feed off this and grow out of control. It's getting worse each summer as waters continue to warm. When there's a large outbreak, it can destroy local marine eco systems, and that shuts down tourism along the coasts—it can cripple Florida's health and economy," Jay said, sternly.

"We know what causes it, and we need to do agriculture more efficiently without so much waste and runoff—you don't want to see what it does down here, Dave … it's tragic! It doesn't have to be like that … we need to do better and take care of our sacred waters," Ashley said, passionately.

DavidPhillipPa

"Oh, I guess we get something like that up in Lake Erie, but ours is different. We get a green algae bloom that does the same thing; it turns the lake into something like green pea soup, and kills all the fish that swim into it. Our farm runoff and pollution from the cities causes it too, and the warming water makes it worse. Our lake is the shallowest of the five Great Lakes, so it heats up faster during summer. It's like a double whammy—lots of runoff and warm, shallow water. It's on our TV news all the time in the summer months. Lake Erie's the busiest and most populated Great Lake, so it's a serious problem now. When it happens, people can't fish, swim, boat, or drink the water when the outbreak hits in the summer months. And like you said, it's a shame.

"Lake Erie's shoreline is a lot different than Florida's; it can have high cliffs, big boulders and brown rocky sand. All along it are huge soaring trees and many nice lighthouses to warn boaters and freighters of the rocky shoreline. It's so beautiful and important to Ohio—we should do more to stop the algae and protect the water," I explained.

"Well, it's good that you're at least aware of it and want to learn more about it, that's smart. We've seen satellite images of Lake Erie when the green algae outbreak is at its worst; it looks like it can turn the entire lake green—that's unbelievable! We're all citizens of this wonderful planet we live on—we all need a healthy Earth to live," Jen said, earnestly.

"If we ever go up to Ohio, we want to see and enjoy your Great Lake—when it's healthy and clean, it sounds wonderful!" Jay said, as Jen and Ashley smiled and agreed.

David Phillip Parks

Then I wondered, "I'm learning so much about Florida now. There's so much fun going on down here, but how do you relax with all the crowds and tourists from everywhere? Is there any quiet or slow times during the year?"

Jay laughed, "About 22 million people live in Florida now, and most live on the coasts, so finding quiet time can be a challenge these days. But, we do have a slower summer season. Actually … you're in it right now!"

"Why is this the slow season? It still looks really busy to me," I said, looking around at the groups of tourists.

"It can get very hot and humid all summer long, and the sun's radiation is stronger in the tropics than up north, so many people feel it's like living in a steamy sauna down here. And the Gulf water goes from refreshing, to hot and salty in the summer. Many people don't like salt water that warm, so a lot go up north to get away from the heat and humidity. Summers are when the beaches are less crowded, and the prices of condos are lower."

"Yeah, the winter months are the crowded busy months, from Thanksgiving to Easter," Jen added. "There's so many people some days, you can't see the sand in the distance—it's ridiculous!"

"So, no matter what time of year, we can always get quiet time just by jumping on our paddle boards and going for a ride during sunset. It's so peaceful then; just the sun, water, fish, seagulls and sky … they're our friends too—they're family! They're part of us, and we love them," Jay admitted, and I'd never heard anyone her age say it like that.

I just looked around and smiled, "Wow, that's how I feel too back home … I've never heard someone say it like that before."

"It's good you appreciate all this; it's really a gift to us all. So, how do you enjoy quiet time back home, Ohio style?!" Ashley wondered, grinning.

"Well, since we live in a less crowded place back home, there's a lot of quiet time if you want it," I explained.

"There's woods and fields all around us; it's very peaceful in different ways all year long. I like when we watch the sunsets, too. They set behind the farmer's hay barn in early spring, and again in late summer, early fall. We like to explore the field, and sometimes my mom and dad will walk out after supper just to see the sunset too. My mom says 'we're sunset chasers!', and my dad will yell 'SUNSET—SUNSET!' just to make us laugh."

"Wow, I can just imagine that! You're lucky to live there, Dave; your family seems special … to appreciate things like that," Jen said, sweetly.

"Yeah, you'd like it too. There's no water, or seagulls though, but rows of berries, soybeans, or corn as far as you can see. And around the edges are woods, rolling hills, wild flowers, and quiet streams—it's really nice!"

"See, Dave, we're ALL sunset chasers—tell your parents that one!" Ashley said, beaming, as Jay and Jen laughed and nodded.

Then I wondered, "Are there any special fun things my family can do on the beach while we're down here?"

"Oh, that's an easy one … we'd all agree on this—if you're new to Siesta Key life, on Sundays, you gotta see the 'Drum Circle' at Siesta Public Beach during sunset. It's definitely a must see!" Ashley said, laughing. "It's NUTS!"

"Why, what happens there?!" I asked.

"Well, we have a huge arts, culture, and music scene down here, and there's a lot of wealthy and famous people living in the area, and it's nice to go to the museums, galleries, and festivals; but sometimes, we just have to cut loose and chill out—that's when we do the Drum Circle. It's the local scene of drummers and percussionists who like to gather during sunset on the weekend, and just bang on drums, trash cans, bongos, kettle drums, cowbells, anything really that'll make a sound. And, a big crowd of dancers always meets there to dance wildly in front of the drummers—it's hysterical to watch—people just having a crazy fun time during a beautiful sunset!" Jay said, energetically.

"Yeah, you won't find anything like it anywhere else," Ashley said, proudly. "Sometimes the crowd grows to thousands of people—all ages, all races, from all over the world … we all become one with the beat at the Drum Circle, Dave! Check it out while you're here, and make sure your family goes—it's a great time! Your mom, dad, and sister sound fun—I think they'd really like it!"

"Yeah, they might even jump in and dance too!" I said, laughing. "My dad can play drums and bongos—back home he says he's the beat master! He'll get those people dance'n— they'll love him! Just give him bongos, a cowbell, anything— he'll say he's the beach master!"

"Oh … that's too funny! We need to see this guy lay'n it down!" Ashley laughed, in disbelief. "Let us know, Dave, we'll be there for sure!"

"I will if I see you again!"

"Ok, so what do you do back home that's exciting and unique to your area? Something that we would like to see if we were there as tourists?" Jen asked.

I thought for a moment, "I'd say the concert at our city's park, for the 4th of July celebration. The Air Force band and choir put on a really good show, with fireworks at the end—I think you'd like that a lot!"

"That sounds nice, what type of music do they play?" Jay asked.

"They play mostly military, patriotic songs, stuff like that. It's a full band with all the instruments, and a big choir. They're famous—they put on a great show! It's the best thing to do on a warm summer evening in our city. And there's also good walking trails in the park. My mom goes to weekly concerts with her friends in other nearby cities, too."

"I like those kinds of outdoor concerts too," Jay said. "I wish they did them more often. But those famous military bands travel around a lot, so you're lucky to get them during the 4th of July. We're proud of our military and support the veterans for their service."

Then Ashley changed the subject back to animals, "So Dave, when you're back home and out in nature, what big animals do you see the most?"

"Well, when I'm on hikes, or looking for wild berries, I'm real quiet, so sometimes if I'm still for a while I can see lots of animals, but the biggest ones I see a lot are the white tailed deer."

"Oh I think they're so graceful and majestic. We don't have as many deer as you do up north. I think most deer in Florida are in the middle of the state, away from the crowded coastal cities," Jen said.

I added, "Our deer can get really big; I've seen some huge ones with really big antlers!"

"Aren't you worried when they're close to you?" Ashley asked.

"Well, I see them a lot, like all year long. I think they get used to seeing me too—it's like we're neighbors of the farmer's field. If I'm bending down pick'n berries in the thick brush, they might not know I'm there if they don't catch my scent. A few times I've stood up and startled them, but they just look at me, raise their tales, snort, and jump away. Some of the big bucks can get aggressive during the rut season when they're looking for doe—I give 'em lots of space during that time, but most of the year, we see small herds of them … they're my friends too.

"And there's a lot of other animal tracks out in the field. Some other bigger animals can be coyote, fox, black bear, bobcat, and even cougar … so, it's good to know what's outside. So what big animal or fish do you see the most down here?"

"Being on the water a lot, we see just about everything like dolphins, sharks, and sting rays, but when we see manatees, it's almost magical!" Jay said, as Jen and Ashley nodded.

"I know what dolphins, sharks, and sting rays are—I want to see some down here, but what's a manatee? I've never heard of those … why's it magical seeing them?" I wondered.

"Well, manatees are the gentle giants caring for our waterways and intracoastals. They're also known as 'sea cows' and they eat, swim, and rest all day. They're friendly and are often curious of people. But, because the big ones can grow to about 13 feet long and weigh over 3,000 lbs., it's amazing to see them up close," Ashley said smiling.

"Why, what happens when they come close? If they're that big, aren't you scared?" I wondered.

"Well, we usually see them during the day, but sometimes, when we're in a lagoon during sunset on our paddle boards, they can silently come up right by us. They're a leathery brown mammal with a cute, squishy face with whiskers, and when they look into our eyes, something magical happens. It's like they're looking into our souls. It's hard to describe in words the feeling we get when it happens … it's like they're asking us to 'take care of them.' They're intelligent, sensitive, and fragile. For all their size, they need a healthy environment to survive—they're depending on us to take care of their world. I guess that's the message we feel when we encounter them like that. We're very lucky and honored to see them in their natural environment."

"Wow, that sounds amazing! I hope someday I see them too, and I'll thank them for caring for our waters," I said, thoughtfully.

ERNST & YOUNG
FLATS
LAKE ERIE 06
DONITAN LANE
David Phillip Parks 2019

Then Ashley wondered, "So, you've been to the big cities up north, do you have a favorite?"

"When my dad has a little vacation, we'll go to one of the big cities near us," I said. "Cleveland, Pittsburgh, or even Columbus. Most of the time we'll go up to Cleveland to a special restaurant and eat outside on a deck overlooking the Cuyahoga River that runs through downtown."

"That sounds interesting, what's that like?" Jen asked.

"Well, there's so much to see and do … like, we're eating a great meal, listening to live music, and a giant freighter goes by that's guided by tugboats, as it winds its way to one of the steel mills or factories along the river. And all these big steel drawbridges have to lift up so the tankers, freighters, and dinner cruises can go up the river, or out to the harbor and Lake Erie. Nearby is First Energy Stadium where the Browns play football, the Rock-n-Roll Hall of Fame Museum, the Great Lakes Science Center, or the observation deck in the Terminal Tower to see the whole city, and the lake. On a nice summer day, it's a great city to see!"

"And it's on a Great Lake!" Ashley jumped in.

"That's right—it's a great city on a great lake!" I laughed. "And if you're up there someday, also go to Cedar Point on Lake Erie—it's one of the best amusement parks in the world!"

"Sounds like fun; maybe we should take a trip up north to Ohio—right girls!" Jay said, happily, as Jen and Ashley nodded and smiled.

"So where should we go for big city stuff before we leave?" I asked, in return.

David Phillip Pa

"We go up to Tampa for big city fun. But, for a smaller city, Sarasota has just about everything a larger city has … without all the traffic jams," Jen admitted.

"We love going to Sarasota Jungle Gardens, the Mote Marine Aquarium, the Ringling Museum, St. Armands Circle, Marina Jack, the Mall at U.T.C, Marie Shelby Botanical Gardens, and the great restaurants downtown. After a busy day, we love a nice meal at O'Leary's Tiki Bar and just relaxing at Bayfront Park. We like people watching at the water fountain park overlooking downtown Sarasota with Marina Jack on the bay and all the beautiful boats and yachts in the distance. Just walking around the paths with the amazing banyan trees, and various palm trees is worth it—and the Dolphin Fountain sculpture is a great place to take pictures. It's so beautiful there; we couldn't ask for more in a smaller city. We're very lucky to live near all this!" Jay said, proudly.

Then Ashley jumped in, "But you also gotta go to our amusement parks too, like, Walt Disney World, Epcot, Universal Studios, and Busch Gardens Tampa. They're all awesome—you'll love'em!"

"That sounds good to me, too! I'm gonna tell my family we should go see those places while we're here. Thanks for telling me all that! We wouldn't know about those places and things to do," I said, gratefully.

"So Dave, I'm thinking you're in maybe 6th grade, am I right?" Jay wondered.

"Yep, that was my grade—I'll be in 7th grade soon—the first week of September," I said, proudly.

She continued, "You seem to like learning new things— that's good! What do you think you'd like to do when you're older?"

"I like studying science and nature at school, but I like to do art too. Maybe I'll be an architect someday, or a Cleveland Browns football player … who knows. I guess I'm too young to know right now—gimme ten years, I'll have a better answer

P12
David Phillip Pankey 2020

for ya!" I laughed and the girls giggled. "So are you going to school for something? What would you like to do in ten years?"

Ashley spoke first, "I'm studying to work maybe at the Mote Marine Laboratory as a marine biologist and help injured animals or marine life—to reintroduce them back into nature safely. I'd be happy doing that!"

"Oh, I think you'd be a good one, Ashley—I can see you helping lots of things!" I said, enthusiastically.

Jen said, "I'm studying to do design work for future sustainable housing near coastal environments … do you know what I mean?"

"Well, is it building better places on water?" I said, a little unsure.

Jen nodded, "Yeah, that's pretty close—it's working with city planners or developers who want to build better housing in areas where flooding is a problem. Floating developments are also new trends overseas, like in Europe and Japan. The environment is changing and we have to change with it—I want to help make that happen. With sea levels rising, it'll be an important field in the future."

"Wow, that sounds interesting—you can do it, Jen!" I said, encouragingly.

Then Jay jumped in, "Well, Dave, my interests are in flying—I'm in a pilot's training program to be a commercial pilot. My dad's a private pilot, so he's helping me. I love flying so I have to figure out what type of aircraft I want to fly. And, I want to travel more and see friends in California. Cali has a lot in common with Florida; some people call it 'Califlorida.' I want to visit there, then Hawaii after that. Maybe I'll be flying a smaller seaplane, or larger private jets—that's my passion!" Jay said, optimistically.

"I think you'd be best pilot in the whole sky, Jay!" I said confidently. "Go check out Califlorida!"

DavidPhillipParks 2020

"Thanks, Dave!" Jay said. "I think we all appreciate your believing in us—we all need to work hard to make our dreams come true, but I think we can do it, right girls?!" making Jen and Ashley smile, "Absolutely—we'll do our best, Dave!"

Then I noticed the sun had crossed the sky and realized we'd all been talking for hours, and I was starting to get hungry. I figured Mom and Dad wanted me back to go eat.

So I waved, "Well, I should get back to my family now, we're going out to eat someplace soon, but I sure have liked meeting all of you—I've never met anyone like you in my life! I learned so many things today—thanks Jay, Jen, and Ashley! I'm gonna go tell my family all about you—hopefully we'll talk again!"

"Oh, you better count on it, Dave! We had a great time too—it was nice learning about your world in Ohio—we hope to run into you again soon!" Jay said, waving.

"Tell your family we say HEY!" Jen happily waved.

"Enjoy your meal with your family, Dave—see ya later!" Ashley waved, smiling.

"I will—see ya later!" I said as I waved goodbye and started walking through the high sea grass along a big sand dune. When I got a ways away, I heard the girls yell, "HEY DAVE! …" and I whirled back around to them as they yelled, "REMEMBER … DRUM CIRCLE!!!" I laughed and gave them a thumbs up and another heart-felt wave of thanks. What a wonderful experience that was; I was so grateful to meet them; to know people like them existed in the world.

David Phillip Park

As I slowly strolled back up the beach, I was thinking of all the things they taught me. It was like I was in an incredible school with all these new ideas they gave me. I started realizing I had so much to learn about the world. So many people were doing so many things around the world that I had no idea about, as well as all the places I'd never seen. Just in one afternoon, I knew this place gave me a gift that opened up my mind.

As I walked, the sun was getting lower in the sky and larger clouds were billowing up and radiated colors of brilliant yellows and oranges, yet other clouds became softer pinks and purples. With the various blues behind them, the sky looked like a amazing painting I'd never seen before. It was mesmerizing and I felt blessed to see it on this tropical island beach. There was so much to think about in this new world.

I came up on another sand dune, and beyond it seagrass and flowers surrounded a palm leaf umbrella with a group of high school students under it. They were all staring at their phones, texting, taking selfies, completely ignoring the amazing colored sky, the sea green Gulf water, and the white sandy beach. I couldn't believe none of them seemed to care about the paradise we were all in, and I felt sorry for them. I wondered if they'd learned anything new during their stay here. Did they meet any special people they had no idea existed? Or was the world inside their phones more important than the one all around them. They could see, but they were so self absorbed, it was also like they were blind. I shook my head to myself, sighed, and walked on past the dune and into the long sea grass leading to our condo.

I looked to the water and saw Mom and Dad were swimming and waved, so I ran into the warm water to meet them as they were coming up to shore.

"Hey, did you have fun on your walk? You've been gone for a long time!" Mom said, cheerfully.

David Phillip Parks 2020

"Boy, I had quite a day!" I chuckled. "How was yours?"

Before Mom could answer, Dad said, "Let's do all this nice chatting over a tasty meal—I'm hungry, Honey … I've been work'n all day!"

"Oh, you've been collecting sea shells, talking to tourists, and floating on your raft all day—that's what your father's been doing, David!" as she and Dad laughed.

Then Katie came running up from the beach that was closer to the condo, "Hey, I met some nice kids from New Jersey … I can't wait to tell you about them!"

"Let's go get cleaned up and talk over dinner—where are we going?" Mom asked all of us.

"The Summerhouse, Turtles, The Boatyard, Magic Moment & Blueberry Hill, Clayton's, Dutch Valley, Cafe Gardens,—ALL OF 'EM!" Dad happily suggested.

We all told our adventures we'd had that day while enjoying delicious Nunzio sandwiches at Cafe Gardens in Siesta Village. And each day afterward at dinner, soothing music, talking, and laughter filled the air, followed by a sunset stroll along the shore. We swam, built sandcastles, rode beach bikes, went sailing on a catamaran, snorkeled off the coral reef, tried kayaking, paddle boarding, and enjoyed the Drum Circle. We made friends with families from England, Sweden, Germany, Italy, South America, Mexico, Asia, and many states across the U.S.

On our last evening after dinner, we went for one more sunset stroll along the Gulf's soothing shore. The sun's rays were spectacular as they spanned the entire sky and reflected off the water as if an embrace of love from nature to us all. We knew we were flying home the next day, and were realizing how much Siesta Key had touched and rejuvenated our souls. I'd seen the girls two more times, and we always had great talks. I was going to miss them, but so glad we met. The friends we all made there, and the experiences we had were always going to be in our hearts.

The next morning, we finished packing our suitcases, had a quick breakfast, and were looking at the Gulf of Mexico's shimmering sea green waters gently caressing the white fluffy sand of Crescent Beach. We were saying goodbye to Siesta Key, when suddenly, a large wild white and yellow parrot landed right near us, and seemed to bid us farewell. It looked at us for a moment, raised its large head feathers, and we gathered around it, amazed.

Dad said, happily, "WOW—look—it's a tropical sweet bird come'n to say goodbye!"

Mom said, surprised, "Oh my, how beautiful! Say goodbye to this tropical little angel!"

And in a moment it spread its wings and gracefully caught the warm breeze coming off the beach and flew away.

"Boy, you don't see THAT everyday … DO YA KIDS?!" Dad said, with a big smile.

We went to touch the sand one last time before climbing into the car.

"Thank you, Siesta Key—we'll be back!" Mom said, gratefully, as we loaded into the car. We drove out onto Midnight Pass Road, smiled back at our building, and drove away. As we went over the Stickney Point drawbridge, we looked back to catch the last glimpses of Siesta Key. Our hearts were swelling with emotion, when Dad rolled down the window and waved, "… We're head'n to FLOHIO!"

I didn't know what he meant, and as we got onto the ramp to go north on Interstate 75, I asked, "Dad … what's Flohio … what's that mean?"

"Son, it means we're take'n a piece of Florida home with us today … it's a part of us now. It's like your friend Jay said someth'n about Califlorida, well we're living in Flohio now … do ya get it?!"

I thought for a moment, then realized what he meant after Mom said, "That saying 'home is where the heart is'—Dad's saying Florida and Ohio are in our hearts now—we have a home in the north and south," holding back tears of joy as she hugged his arm.

"What do ya think Honey, we're go'n home to Flohio!" Dad said, grinning proudly.

We watched Sarasota fade in the distance and passed through Bradenton, then headed back over the Sunshine Skyway Bridge to the other side of Tampa Bay and to St. Petersburg. Everything we saw and experienced: the clusters of palm trees, the pelicans gliding over the water, the salt water scent hanging in the humid air, the sailboats sailing across the bay, the tropical flowers, the sand-lined coves, the banyan trees … they all passed by the window, and had special meaning now.

As we pulled onto the palm-lined causeway leading to the Tampa International Airport, we circled around it and watched some jets take off and powerfully climb into the deep blue sky of south Florida, and head to countless places over the horizon, with us joining them soon.

Arriving at the airport gave us a chance to see how big it actually was. Its design and layout were very different from Pittsburgh's airport. After checking our luggage, we had to find the right tram to get to the proper terminal gate.

David Phillip P

Walking through the airport was very interesting. I couldn't believe how big it was; it was like its own city! There were so many people going everywhere—it was very exciting to be there!

I felt proud that we'd had a wonderful vacation in Florida, and hoped all these other people had the same. Dad told me not all the travelers were flying for vacations; many of them needed to fly for work, reunions, school, weddings—everything you could imagine people needed to do. They were all relying on countless airports all over the world to get them to their destinations safely, and quickly. He said millions did it everyday … I couldn't imagine that!

We eventually got to our tram, loaded inside, and were whisked away on an above ground track to the smaller terminal that held all the gates. The tram was packed with people and went fast and banked just like a roller coaster. Dad was sitting with Mom and looked at Katie and me with really big eyes while he grinned—the same look he would do on a roller coaster back home. It was a funny face, and he didn't care if other people saw him, he did it just to crack us up and relax us.

The tram arrived at the gate terminal quickly, and we got off as more people waited to get on. We headed over to an area to eat a quick snack, then went to the restroom to freshen up, and then over to a large seating area at the gates. All the chairs were taken by passengers waiting to go back to Pittsburgh with us.

"These people could live near us back home!" I realized.

"That's right," Dad agreed. "These people could live all around the Pittsburgh region."

Mom added, "Maybe some went down to Siesta Key too!" After a quick scan, I realized nobody looked familiar. We found some seats, and Mom and Katie sat down and had lots to talk about, while Dad and I wanted to look around some more.

We went up to the huge windows that faced the airplanes on the tarmac, the airfield, runways, and downtown Tampa in the distance. We really liked watching everything going on outside. I'd never seen any of that before and pointed straight ahead, "Look Dad, is that our plane? It's HUGE! And look at all those workers doing their jobs—Wow!"

"Yep, that's our plane!" he said, with pride.

He showed me what each person was doing and how each job was important, "See that guy down there, he's gonna load our luggage into the side of the plane—our bags are on that cart. And look over there … that one's connecting a power cord to charge the plane's batteries. And look at how the passenger tunnel extends over to the plane; it's on wheels and is driven over to the plane's door—it's flexible with each plane cuz some planes are shorter, others are bigger and higher—the tunnel can adjust to all that!"

He continued, "There's waste trucks, food delivery trucks, and look, you can see the pilots in the cockpit getting their flight instructions and instruments ready for the flight. Remember, that plane fully loaded is about 170,000 lbs. A lot of people work hard to get that off the ground—go over 500mph, 40,000 feet—and in about 2 hours, back down in Pittsburgh … and do it all day, everyday—safely! And check out those jet engines—that's serious power there! And look, there's a jet take'n off now!" as we heard the roar of the jet climbing into the sky. "Ya don't see that everyday … do ya kid?!" as he chuckled to himself. He was right, I'd never seen that many interesting things all in one view, in my whole life!

I noticed in the distance that thunderstorms were growing fast, "Look Dad, do you think we're fly'n through storms later?"

"I'm not sure; we'll find out soon 'cuz I think we'll be boarding in a little bit. Let's go back to your mother and Katie and get our stuff ready."

Just then, a nice woman picked up the intercom and gave us instructions, "If all flyers departing for Pittsburgh could please get in line, do so now … we'll be boarding in about five minutes, thank you very much!"

We took another good look at everything, and I realized people in line were hugging loved ones, friends, and co-workers goodbye, as were many people in other lines at the other gates all around ours. Some people seemed happy, others seemed sad, as they all boarded their planes. I hoped they all had good flights.

In a moment we got into line and went to the ticket agent as she smiled and scanned our tickets, saying cheerfully, "Have a great flight!" We thanked her and walked down the passenger tunnel to the plane.

We followed the line of people into the plane, and I heard fans running, and saw flight attendants loading small carts. As we walked near the cockpit door, I got a quick peek and glimpsed the backs of the pilots in their seats—turning dials, pushing buttons and flipping switches. Katie and I sat in front of Mom and Dad again, and I got the window seat at the wing again; a good spot for watching everything.

I was an experienced flyer now, so I was more familiar with the routine, and as we fastened our seat belts, I glanced at Katie, "I got my crackers … I'm ready—you got yours?"

"No, you can have mine—I think I'll have the snacks and drink pop later," she grinned.

Just then the plane began moving backwards. I learned a small, stout vehicle was pushing the plane away from the gate; and even though I couldn't see it, I knew it was under the nose of the plane.

Soon after, the vehicle let go of the plane's front gear, and drove away. Then the jet engines revved higher and we started going down the runway. I was facing the airport and glad we'd had a nice experience, and watched it leave the view of the window. The plane then turned to the left and rounded a bend. Dad leaned forward so we could hear him, "Get ready—here we go …"

Without stopping, the plane turned left again and the engines spooled up to full power and a muffled roar could be heard as our bodies were pressed backwards into our seats. Dad leaned forward again, "Hold on to your cookies, Kids!" as he and Mom chuckled again.

The engine roar climbed higher in pitch and the distant trees, hangars, and Tampa skyline quickly left our view as we sped down the runway. As everything was racing by faster, the plane pitched up and the tires left the ground, and the smooth feeling of air lifted us up above the busy tropical city.

Within a minute, we climbed through the low clouds and I looked back to see downtown Tampa fade away in the distance, with the bay stretching out to the horizon. Thick clouds suddenly obscured my view of the city, and we continued to climb, then leveled off a little. We were expecting the seatbelt sign to turn off, but it stayed on as the plane began hitting some turbulence.

Katie decided to read a fun book of puzzles, mazes, word games, and memory quizzes. I decided it was time to break out my little bag of crackers, bottled water, and enjoy the views of the thick towering clouds zipping past the window.

After some time, I noticed the ground was mostly blocked by heavy clouds and seemed far below us, when the flight attendant announced we were at the cruising altitude of 40,000 feet, and they would soon be offering snacks and drinks.

Katie enjoyed her peanuts and pop, and I was happy with my crackers and water. People around us were reading, talking, and laughing, when the pilot's voice came on and warned us of strong turbulence ahead. In a few moments, the plane suddenly lurched up, then down. Several minutes later, it did it again, but the lurching went on for a while. I looked out the window at the wingtip; it was moving up and down more.

We were now entering a region of larger thunderheads, which were growing in height, and were now much higher than our plane was flying.

We flew for quite some time, going around many storms and hitting pockets of turbulence along the way. After some more time passed, the storms separated enough so that the countryside below became visible.

Dad also noticed, "Hey look—I think we're somewhere near the Ohio River … I think the pilots are fly'n around the big storms."

Some of the thunderstorms grew to a certain height, then their tops spread out like a huge table and were very baggy underneath, that Dad called mammatus clouds. Soon, I saw lightning streaking throughout the storms.

The turbulence became worse once the storms grew together into a continuous massive storm system. Katie and I looked at each other worried when the plane bounced hard, and Dad leaned up to the back of my seat, "You two do'n ok?" as he and Mom figured we were getting nervous as the plane continued to buck up and down, "This is normal storm turbulence," he said, reassuringly.

Suddenly, the plane hit intense turbulence, bouncing up and rolling side to side before plunging down, lifting us up out of our seats. I tightened my seatbelt more, leaned over to the window, and asked him quietly so other passengers couldn't hear, "Dad … the bumps are get'n stronger, is the plane gonna be ok?!"

Mom heard me, and calmly said, "Don't worry, we'll be through it soon." A moment later, the plane rocked wildly, making people gasp out loud. I could hear some people whispering nervously, trying to comfort themselves. I saw the wings bounce more as they sliced through the darkening, boiling clouds lit up by the ongoing lightning.

David Phillip Parks 2020

I leaned back to the window, and said quietly, "Geez … Dad … are the wings gonna break … do you see them bouncing?"

He leaned forward again, "They're suppose to do that—they can bend way more …" but as he said that the plane dropped as if on a hill of a giant rollercoaster, making him and many others yelp in surprise, as he blurted out to Mom, "Wow … that was a big one, Honey—I'm shut'n up!"

We heard and felt thunder booming over the roaring engines. The plane leveled off and gradually the engines began winding down.

After some time passed, Mom said,"Well it seems like we've been descending for a while now—we're on our approach to the airport. Hopefully we'll break through this soon."

Dad agreed, "Yeah, I think we're slowing down too, my ears are start'n to pop—gimme some more gum."

Katie and I decided to chew gum too—it really helped my ears not hurt so much while we descended. I wasn't able to look out the window for a while because the rain and hail mix was too heavy against the window. After a while, a flight attendant announced, "We'll be landing in Pittsburgh in about 15 minutes, please make sure your seat belts are fastened, and personal belongings are secured."

Within a few minutes, the plane broke through the clouds and I was briefly able to see the airport, runways, and parking lots below; we were all relieved to be close to home now. I saw the control tower and realized there was a team of air traffic controllers guiding our pilots through the storms all this time. I felt a deep sense of gratitude and respect for them, and as the airport came closer, I felt pilots were very brave people.

The plane banked to the right and we lowered out of the cloud base, and the landing gear began lowering and locking into position as we made our final approach.

David Phillip Parker

As the landscape and rolling hillsides of Pittsburgh got closer, I saw the many freeways and traffic come into view. The storms were moving on, and in the distance I saw downtown bathed in sunlight with heavy rain beyond it. Soon, the tires touched down, and the reverse thrust engaged, making our bodies lurch forward in our seats; and as the runway passed by the window more slowly, I think we all thanked God to be safely on the ground. As the plane taxied to the gate terminal, a relieved flight attendant came on, "Welcome to Pittsburgh, you may unbuckle your seat belts now. Please stay seated until the plane arrives at the gate. We hope you enjoy your stay in Pittsburgh—have a great day!"

When we arrived at the gate, there seemed to be a collective 'sigh of relief' from the passengers as we unbuckled our seat belts, stood up, and got in line to exit the plane. Dad looked at us relieved, and with big eyes said, "Boy—that was someth'n else! How'd you like to fly us through all that?! … You gotta be the MAN to fly through all those storms, I tell ya!", when the cockpit door opened and a beautiful red-haired, blue-eyed woman pilot stepped out.

She smiled, "Welcome to Pittsburgh—I'm sorry for the bumpy ride we had back there!"

Dad noticed her four stripes on her shoulders, "Are you the Captain?! Did you just fly us home?!"

She look confidently at us and said, grinning, "Yes I am—and yes I did!" which made us all smile—enjoying her quick wit and cheerful demeanor.

Mom said, gratefully, "You both did an excellent job … thank you for getting us home safely!"

She smiled, nodding, "That was a challenge—we avoided the biggest storms by following the Ohio River into the region. Some of those storms may've produced tornadoes."

"We flew through tornadoes?!" Dad asked, shocked.

"Well, not through them, but around them. We're continuing on to Philadelphia in an hour, then down to Atlanta later tonight," as we all said "Wow" in admiration for her bravery and skills.

Her male co-pilot quickly stood up and left the cockpit with her. They walked ahead of us up the tunnel, reviewing notes of their upcoming flight and the weather. Once we emerged to the gate seating in the terminal, she glanced back at us, smiled and waved, "Have a good day—we'll see you soon!" We waved and were grateful to have her as our Captain.

As they walked away from us, I realized that Jay might be walking with them someday as a Captain too—how incredible that would be! I was inspired knowing they were all following their dreams. When we turned to walk away, some other pilots passed us, smiled and joked, "Welcome to Cleveland!" as we all laughed and continued on our way to the underground tram.

Just before we got to the tram, we noticed a large dinosaur skeleton of a Tyrannosaurus Rex at the end of the escalators, so we had fun taking pictures of it with a nice family from India who were also admiring its fearsome size. It looked very interesting as it towered over our heads, and we imagined how it looked as it roamed across pre-historic earth.

"You think you could outrun that thing?!" Dad asked, sarcastically. "You'd end up as a snack!" he chuckled loudly; and Mom playfully smacked his arm, "Oh Honey!"

As we loaded into the tram, he teased her, "You'd be a snack too!" making us laugh as we stood holding on to a support bar in the crowded tram car.

We quickly zipped through the underground tunnel, and soon arrived at the main terminal, where we got our luggage at the baggage carousel. Now that we had all of our luggage, we relaxed and had fun looking at all the people busily walking around the main terminal lobby, and Mom asked, "So kids, what did you think of your first round-trip flight?"

"I thought it was exciting!" Katie said, happily.

I took a moment, "Well, go'n to Tampa was smooth … but come'n back was like a long storm chase up in the sky … I was get'n pretty scared!"

"Well, your mother got scared too!" Dad said, laughing.

Mom chuckled and shot back, "Oh Phil, you held on to the armrests so tightly your knuckles turned white!"

Dad grinned because he knew she was right, and playfully said, "That whole flight was FANTASTICO! Alright, let's go get the car and head home!"

As we left the terminal, we looked back at it, and Mom said, enthusiastically, "Just think of all we've seen and done in these past two weeks since we were here last—it's amazing!"

"Sure has … now all we gotta do is find the car!" Dad said jokingly as we ventured into the sea of cars and trucks at the long term parking lot. We eventually found our car and got onto the expressway to leave the airport. As we got onto the freeway and headed north, a large passenger jet flew right over us as it took off into the sky, "WOW … I wonder where they head'n?!" Dad said, with wonder and enthusiasm. "Just think—we all just did THAT!" making us all smile.

After we maneuvered through the heavy traffic, we began seeing the many special and unique features of western Pennsylvania with its large, velvety green hills, something not seen in Florida. While approaching a large steel bridge that crossed the Ohio River, we noticed the distant river towns with their smoke stacks gently billowing into the clearing sky.

David Phillip Pe

Gliding below the massive bridge was a large river towboat pushing a barge loaded with slag, gravel, and coal, and was now beneath us and heading down the river.

Mom saw it first, "Hey, look at the tugboat barge passing under us!"

Dad then noticed, "It's headed to all the mills and factories down river. That's probably a towboat pushing that barge—it's not as big as the cruise ship we saw, but that tow boat pushes those heavy barges all over the place! Ya don't see THAT everyday … DO YA, KIDS!?"

He then described how all the raw materials went to the mills, plants, and factories to be made into concrete, cement, and steel that makes the modern world possible.

Dad explained, "All those highways we drove on and buildings we passed on the trip, the cars and trucks—this is where they begin—as piles of rock and iron ore on barges and trains. Our region makes the materials used in all of that, and then manufactures those things too—something to appreciate, respect, and be proud of, kids!" I thought about how I make things with my LEGOs, and how adults make everything in real life. Seeing the towboat barge made me realize that.

As we crossed the bridge, I wondered what all the river town's people were doing. Then I noticed a large jet that had taken off from the airport 15 miles back, and wondered if some of those people left their homes, and were flying over, going to a new and distant place. As we got closer to Ohio, the hills became more gentle, and were separated by large fields of corn and soybean. I was remembering how different it was to Florida.

We soon crossed over the state line, and saw a comforting sight: 'Welcome To Ohio—the Buckeye State!' It was fun pointing out familiar places and things to each other, "Look—there's our school!" and, "Look—there's the grocery store!" We were very happy to be back home!

When we pulled onto our street, our neighborhood was still the same wonderful place, but we had changed. Our world had grown, and as we pulled into our driveway, we knew our home was a special little piece of a much bigger world. I had a much better understanding of that now. We eagerly looked around at everything that was so familiar, and yet now seemed new.

Dad pulled up to the garage, turned off the car and we excitedly jumped out just to look around with awe.

"We made it, Honey—WHAT A TRIP!" Dad announced, proudly.

"It sure was incredible!" Mom reflected, capturing all our feelings. As we gazed at our beautiful yard, the stately trees, and colorful flowers, a hawk flew in the distance and we felt a part of it—we were now sky beings too!

Katie and I hugged Mom and Dad knowing they worked so hard to make that amazing trip possible, "Thanks so much Mom and Dad for taking us—what a wonderful vacation we had!" Katie said, gratefully.

"We love you so very much!" I said, with all my heart.

They smiled and hugged us lovingly.

"Well, we thought it was time for you to see some other places!" Mom said, intuitively.

Dad added, "Yeah—the world's a big place … we gotta get out there—AND DO IT!" making a funny face and cracking us up.

"Ok, lets get the luggage inside and unpack," Mom suggested. "There's no food in the house; we should go shopping for groceries."

David Phillip Parks

"It's been a big day, Honey … I think I'm gonna catch the news, and take a nap first," Dad said yawning, "I feel a good one come'n on!" That seemed like a good idea, so after we brought the luggage in, Dad went to his favorite chair, Mom and Katie went upstairs to freshen up and unpack, while I watched the news with Dad, then took a nap on the couch.

The news was covering an Indians (future Cleveland Guardians) and Pirates game when I woke up, and Dad was still napping peacefully in his chair. I thought about the news we would watch in Florida, and seeing highlights of the Marlins and Devil Rays. I smiled to myself of how people root for their teams while loving the same sports.

I then wondered what my neighborhood friends were doing. So I went outside and glanced up and down the street; some were playing basketball up the street, a few were riding bikes down the street, while others were playing kickball in a front yard … about the same as two weeks ago.

I decided to check out the backyard and beyond to see the farmer's field. It was a balmy summer evening, and the sun bathed the field and woods in a warm glow. I walked out into the field and sat at the base of my oak tree and was happy seeing the emerald green soybean crop, the wild flowers, the soaring hawks, the gentle rolling wooded hills, the endless blue sky, and I felt grateful. Even though two weeks had gone by, everything was just the same as when I'd left. But I felt different sitting there under the tree, and was realizing how big the world actually is, and I was just a tiny part of it.

What I thought I knew before was now just a speck of understanding. I had no idea of how amazingly diverse the world was: the people, the cultures, the places, the wildlife. It was absolutely incredible to be a part of all of that. I wondered what Jay, Jen, and Ashley were doing, and how lucky I was to have known them—we shared our worlds with one another. And even though northeast Ohio is very different than southwest Florida, we all learned to understand, appreciate, and celebrate the differences, knowing that's what makes life interesting and special. I hoped they were happy and lived their dreams.

Then I thought about how amazing it was to fly. The training, skill, and dedication of the pilots, to the air traffic controllers that guide them safely to their destinations each day. Then to the aeronautical engineers and mechanics who build and maintain every plane on every flight; and the friendly, hard-working airport employees who make sure everything runs smoothly at the many airports. And all the millions of people flying each day; I didn't realize this was a normal part of people's lives outside my little town.

And now I had new memories of the tropics and the sea to think about. The world's oceans are so much larger than anything I'd known. I saw new types of animals and marine life, from the colorful wild parrots squawking in the giant banyan trees, the darting little lizards and geckos, the diving pelicans, the fragile egrets, the playful dolphins, the elusive sharks and sting rays, to the gentle manatees.

I was amazed at all the many kinds of palm trees, flowers, and Spanish moss that draped from the trees; I'd never seen any of that before. And the beautiful white, fluffy quartz sands of Siesta Key's beaches, to the magnificent Gulf of Mexico's warm sea green salty waters, and how they reflected the colorful skies during a sunset, its gentle waves and breezes giving life to all of nature in the tropics. And all the various people drawn to its beauty, from all parts of the world. To see how people smile while strolling the beach or playing in the water, it didn't matter which country they came from, the Gulf's waters made us all one family.

Then I thought of Mom and Dad and how they made it all possible. I learned that everything we did required money: the flights, the condo, the meals, even the bikes, rafts, and paddle boards—they all cost money. We couldn't have done any of it without them working hard every year to save up for their dream vacation. All they asked of us kids was to do our best at school, do our house chores each week, and be respectful of others. I learned not to take their efforts for granted and appreciate all they've done for us.

I looked around the field again, stood up, and was proud. I carried both northern fields and tropical sandy beaches in my soul now, and as I walked back home, I wanted to tell my family what I learned that day; but I knew they were feeling the same way: that life is about learning, loving, caring, and working towards a goal.

Several weeks had passed and our life in Ohio got back to a normal mid-summer routine. But our time in Florida really influenced us, and we made some changes in honor of our Florida experience. So Mom decided we should have colorful tropical flowers on the kitchen walls and artwork she brought from Siesta Key throughout the house.

One evening, Dad was thinking about the large parrot we'd seen before we left Florida, "Honey, I've been think'n 'bout how that parrot visited us—maybe we should get a sweet bird for a pet!"

Mom said, "Ok, as long as it's a small one."

David Phillip Parks 2020

So one day, they got a baby parakeet and named him 'Budgie.' Budgie quickly became part of our family, and one of his favorite things to do was to fly around and visit each of us.

One day after Dad got home from work, he was sitting at the table looking forward to supper, with Budgie talking to his ear. As Budgie talked away, Dad had some more ideas, "Honey, we sure had a great time in Florida! I'm think'n we should go on another vacation—somewhere TROPICAL again!"

Mom was making sweet corn, and enjoyed hearing his enthusiasm, and thought he was kidding around, "Honey, we just got BACK from the tropics! … So what did you have in mind this time?!" she asked, curiously.

"Well since we're living in Flohio now, let's think bigger next time. Let's try HAWAII next … what do ya think?!"

Mom was shocked and smiled as she turned to bring the corn over, "Honey … that's a BIG TRIP! That's on the other side of the world from us!" she giggled.

Once I heard that, I got out the globe, a map, and began searching for Hawaii with Katie pointing on the globe, "Look, it's way over here in the Pacific Ocean!"

"Now THAT would be a vacation … LET'S DO IT!" Dad said loudly, making Budgie chirp loudly. "If we mixed Hawaii with Ohio, that would be 'HAWIO' … or maybe 'OHAII'—which one sounds better?!" he said, laughing.

Mom said happily, "We'll start saving for next year, Honey—right now, we're LIVING IN FLOHIO!"

We couldn't agree more!

About the Author/Illustrator

David Phillip Parks is the author/illustrator of the children's book, "Weather … It Matters," the co-author (with Elizabeth Streb Parks) and illustrator of "David's Castle On Crescent Beach," the illustrator of Elizabeth Streb Parks' books, "Kevie Keanu's Walk With Nana," and "My Dad Was So Mean," co-author (with Marlene McKnight Koenig) and illustrator of "Frisky Wins His Heart."

Besides writing/illustrating, David's involved in a variety of pursuits: plays several musical instruments (mainly drums), inventing/applied mechanical engineering, welding/metal-working, athletics and nature. Having lived in both Ohio and Florida, he studied at a state university and is a Meteorologist/storm spotter, specializing in severe weather and field research in tornado development.